THE
HUNKY-DORY
DAIRY

ANNE LINDBERGH, daughter of Charles and Anne Morrow Lindbergh, is a short story writer, poet, and author of five previous novels. Ms. Lindbergh has been writing for as long as she can remember. In all of her books, she prefers "taking children—who could be the readers—ordinary children in ordinary life and having something happen that gets them into an extraordinary situation.... I hope that my books are an invitation to invent."

THE HUNKY-DORY DAIRY

Anne Lindbergh

Illustrated by Julie Brinckloe

AN AVON CAMELOT BOOK

AVON BOOKS
A division of
The Hearst Corporation
1790 Broadway
New York, New York 10019

The Harcourt Brace Jovanovich edition contains the following Library of Congress
Cataloging in Publication Data:

Lindbergh, Anne.
  The hunky-dory dairy.

  Summary: Eleven-year-old Zannah befriends the residents of a dairy that has been
removed by magic from the nineteenth to the twentieth century.
  [1. Space and time—Fiction. 2. Magic—Fiction. 3. Friendship—Fiction.
4. Washington (D.C.)—Fiction] I. Brinckloe, Julie, ill. II. Title.
PZ7.L6572Hu   1986   [Fic]   85-16408

First Camelot Printing: May 1987

For Lizzie and Zannah, Anne and Wendy,
Connie F. and Connie P., and any other daughters
who run their mothers' lives

LIST OF ILLUSTRATIONS

THE
HUNKY-DORY
DAIRY

I T RAINED on Patty's birthday.

I lay in bed and listened to the drops hitting the gutter outside my window. They made a steady drumming sound, like rain that's there to stay. The alarm hadn't gone off yet, and Patty was still asleep. I lay wondering what it was like to be Patty, and whether she would mind the rain.

Patty was thirty-one that morning: just twenty years older than me. I felt more like her little sister than her daughter. As for my father, I never had one to speak of. He was killed in a car accident just before I was born. Patty and I had lived alone together ever since, but I had been trying to get her married again to someone—*anyone*—ever since I could remember. I wanted to get us out of our tiny house and our tiny neighborhood, and Patty's dreary job running the Tiny Fingers Preschool Playgroup and tearing her hair over it every night.

I had a present for Patty, all wrapped and ribboned on my bedside table. It was a pocket calculator—to save her pride.

Patty could add, subtract, and multiply in the supermarket like any other grown-up, but when it came to the Tiny Fingers Playgroup her mind went blank. Parents would give her one-fifty for the field trip and three-twenty-five for the class photo, and complain that they had overpaid twelve cents a week for milk all year. Then Patty's big brown eyes would grow all soft and fuzzy and she would say, "Oh, I'm so sorry! I'll check with my records and get back to you about it tomorrow." Since Patty's records consisted of crumpled-up scraps of paper in her purse, she would go home and tear her hair. Only now she wouldn't have to, because I had saved up for a calculator.

But it was raining. A pocket calculator didn't seem festive enough for a rainy birthday. I wished I could offer Patty the moon, or a cruise to the Bahamas, or the perfect man. I wished I could offer her her heart's desire.

Jumping out of bed, I ran into her room, hugged the long shape wrapped in a sheath of blankets, and said, "Happy birthday, Patty! If you could have your heart's desire, what would it be?"

Patty moaned sleepily and answered, "A quart of milk and the *Washington Post*."

That's how it all began.

CHAPTER 1

Patty WENT BACK to sleep, and the rain came down harder than ever. I hoped for her sake that it stopped by nine o'clock, when twelve mothers and fathers would arrive with twelve preschoolers at the Tiny Fingers Playgroup in Saint Michael's Church.

On wet days the Tinies came equipped with boots, raincoats, and umbrellas, and Patty would go into a dither. The boots were the worst: Patty simply couldn't keep them straight. She had been known to send a Tiny home wearing two left boots, each of which belonged to another Tiny.

For the moment, the rain showed no sign of stopping. It was so dark outside that I checked the clock again to make sure it was really six o'clock and not earlier. Burleith, which is our part of Washington, D.C., is full of tall trees. I'm grateful for their shade in summer, but when it rains you don't get much light in row houses like ours.

I pulled on jeans and a sweatshirt, grabbed a piece of raisin bread, dropped my book bag near the front door where I wouldn't forget it on my way to school, and ran. I had an umbrella, but I knew it wouldn't do me any good; Washington rain bounces back up from the pavement. The supermarket was four blocks away and by the time I got back home with the milk and the paper, umbrella or not, I was sure to be soaked to the bone.

It was October and the leaves had turned, but even the gaudiest maple leaves looked dreary in the rain. I decided to buy flowers for Patty at the market. Roses would be nice. I could imagine her screaming when I walked through the door with thirty-two roses, one for each year of her life and one to grow on. I could imagine her hugging me, roses and all. Unfortunately I couldn't afford thirty-two roses. The most I could afford was three.

My head was full of roses as I ran across the supermarket parking lot and slammed right into the automatic door. The reason it didn't open when I stepped on the rubber matting was that it was too early. The market was shut.

I could have kicked myself for being such a dreamer. Why hadn't I stayed warm and dry in our kitchen and made Patty a practical surprise, like pancakes for breakfast? Grumbling aloud and feeling very sorry for myself, I sloshed through the rain toward home. It was so dark under the trees that the street lights were still on. Their reflection glowed in the puddles, and it felt more like night than day. In that kind of weather, anyone with sense stays in bed with a book.

What would be the best way to convince Patty to let me skip school: pathos? Like, "I never seem to have you to myself these days, Patty. Could we celebrate your birthday by spending the day together—just the two of us?"

Or how about bravado: "Give yourself a break, Patty. You only live once. Schools are for fools—we're staying home today!"

And Patty would agree like a shot. She'd perk right up and say—

My daydream was interrupted by a loud whinny near my left ear. I jumped about a foot. Pulled up to the curb between a motorcycle and a Honda Civic was an old-fashioned horse and van.

At first I thought I must be hallucinating. Wiping the rain

Pulled up to the curb between a motorcycle and a Honda Civic was an old-fashioned horse and van.

out of my eyes, I blinked and looked again. The only time I had seen horses in our neighborhood before was when the park police went by, but this was no police horse. It was a fat old dapple-gray mare, looking very gloomy in the rain. The van that she was harnessed to had recently been given a fresh coat of white paint, and on the side in large blue letters with curlicues all around was printed:

HUNKY-DORY DAIRY
Milk, Butter, & Eggs

Later I wondered why I had been so obsessed with that quart of milk. I knew it wasn't really Patty's heart's desire. I knew she wouldn't mind if I came home without it. But something in my head kept repeating, "Milk = Happy Birthday," and my last hope was that van.

I looked around for the milkman, but there wasn't a soul in sight. Could he be inside his van, sitting out the rain? The door was open at the back, so I climbed in. It was too dark to see much, but it seemed empty. Then, before I had time to climb out again, the door swung shut and the van jerked forward, throwing me to the floor.

Luckily I wasn't hurt, but once I was down there, I decided to stay because I didn't want to fall again. Inching my way cautiously to the side of the van, I sat against the wall, wedged between two carriers of empty milk bottles.

My head was spinning, I felt so scared. Ever since I was old enough to understand, Patty had drilled me about never getting into strange cars with strange men. Even if the milkman turned out to be a woman, the van was as strange as you could get, and where was it taking me? I didn't dare jump out. I didn't even dare yell and hammer on the walls. I just sat there waiting for the van to stop again, but it seemed to go on forever.

As my eyes grew accustomed to the dark, I began to distinguish things around me. Besides the bottles that clinked and clattered so much that I was amazed they didn't break, there was a large box of three-inch roofing nails, two jars of sorghum molasses, two bars of soap, a dozen long, red candles frosted with glitter, a five-pound bag of coffee beans, and a peanut butter sandwich. Everything looked new except the sandwich, which was missing one bite.

A single slice of raisin bread doesn't go far as breakfast. When I saw the sandwich my stomach began to rumble and before I knew what I was doing, I had reached out and taken a second bite. Then I looked at it guiltily. I hadn't left very much sandwich and whoever it belonged to was sure to notice. I stuffed the rest into my cheek and was on the point of destroying the evidence when the van gave a sudden jolt and stopped.

I shivered. My cheekful of peanut butter turned into a tasteless lump but I choked it down hurriedly, expecting the door to fly open and an angry milkman to tell me exactly what he thought of stowaways who ate his snacks.

Nothing happened. The mare whinnied again, and I heard a man's voice talking, and some children answering him. Pushing the door open a crack I peeked out, but the voices came from the front end of the van. All I could see from the back was a grassy slope leading to a pond.

At first the only sign of life was a duck swimming on the pond, but then I saw a face. It hovered over the pond upside down and belonged to a little boy who was dangling by his knees from the branch of a birch tree. The boy was motionless for a second or so. Then, with a wild lurch, he made a grab for the duck. The duck escaped, but the boy plunged headfirst into the pond.

I laughed in spite of myself, but a moment later I caught my breath. The boy was splashing helplessly, and his head kept going under. It was obvious that he couldn't swim. I threw the door wide open, scrambled out of the van, and dashed toward the pond.

The water was freezing, but I didn't even notice until I had clutched the boy by the collar and dragged him to the bank. He seemed no worse for the wear, but I felt terrible. The pond was stagnant and there was foul-smelling mud up to my knees, to say nothing of the fact that my clothes were sopping wet. I was wringing the water out of my sweatshirt when a voice behind me shouted:

"Holy smoke! Loyal Graybeal, what will you think of next?"

I spun around to find myself facing a tall, gangly fellow with sandy hair and sideburns, and a knobby nose that leaned more toward one cheek than the other. A pair of bright blue eyes gleamed out from the shadow of a dark blue cap with "H.D. Dairy" printed on the visor.

H.D. Dairy? He must be the milkman. Now I was in for trouble!

For the moment, however, the milkman was smiling. "Fantastic rescue!" he told me, panting and wiping his forehead with a big white handkerchief. "I suppose we should be grateful, but it would serve him right if you had let him drown. Loyal is the worst child I've ever known for getting into trouble. Who are you, by the way?"

"Zannah McFee," I said.

I was looking over his shoulder at a girl who had come running down the slope to join him. She was about my age, and dressed in an odd, old-fashioned style, as if she had been acting in a play. Judging by all the cuffs and hems that straggled out from under her long, brown dress, she was wearing too many clothes for comfort, but she was barefoot. So, I observed, was Loyal.

"Friend of yours, Utopia?" the milkman asked.

She shook her head. "I thought she came with you."

Utopia and the boy named Loyal both drew closer and stared.

Being too cold and wet to bother with excuses, I told the truth. "That's right," I confessed. "I was in the van."

The milkman was astonished. "In the van?" he repeated. "In *my* van? Holy smoke! I never dreamed it could bring in visitors. But how are we going to get you out again?"

My heart sank. Unless he gave me a ride home I'd have to walk, and by the time I got there, Patty would be out of her mind with worry.

Utopia tugged at my arm. "Don't fuss her with questions, Mr. Pratt. Can't you see she's shivering? I'll take her up to my room and find some dry clothes. You come too, Loyal, or you'll catch your death."

Utopia's room was tiny. The whole house was small, in fact: only a cottage, separated by a muddy yard from the big white barn next door. Utopia had led me dripping wet through a bare, clean-smelling kitchen and up a narrow flight of stairs to a room half the size of mine at home, and this had two beds.

"Loyal sleeps here, too," she told me. "Father is moving him up to the attic room though, as soon as he can find some glass panes for the attic window. He says Loyal is too old to be tied to his sister's apron strings, but I don't think that's fair, do you?"

"How old is he?" I asked.

Utopia sighed dramatically. "Eight, going on nine. I'm three years older, so you'd think I'd be the one to get a room of my own. But of course that would never occur to Father. He thinks girls are of no account."

Putting myself in her place, I tried to imagine what it would be like to want a room of my own. Personally, I had spent my whole life wishing I had a sister or brother to share with. "But you'll have *this* room to yourself now, won't you?" I pointed out. "Isn't that just as good?"

Utopia sighed again. "Yes, well—I only hope no harm comes to Loyal, with no one to keep an eye on him. Why, as soon as I turned my back this morning, he fell into the pond! And last week it was the horse trough, and the week before it was the pickle barrel. Have you ever heard of such a thing? Every inch of him smelled of brine for days, except his feet. They just smelled of feet, but that's to be expected."

I couldn't help giggling. "What's a pickle barrel? You mean a whole barrel full of pickles? You must eat a lot of pickles in your family!"

Utopia stared as if I were out of my mind. "We eat about as much as most folks, I guess, and a barrel's the best thing I know for putting up pickles. What do *you* use?"

I started to explain that Patty and I bought pickles in the small-sized jar at the supermarket, if we bought them at all. We're not that fond of pickles. But I could tell that Utopia wasn't listening: she was too busy pulling clothes out of a wooden chest at the foot of her bed.

The clothes looked peculiar but I was cold, so I stripped off my wet things and put on whatever she handed me. There was a white dress first. It looked like what I wear myself in summer, but Utopia said it was only a petticoat, and made me wear another dress on top. The second one was brown like hers. It scratched and had too many buttons.

"It must take you ages to get dressed in the morning," I said, my fingers fumbling as I tried to do myself up. "Buttons are pretty, but give me a plain old zipper, any day."

"What's a zipper?" asked Utopia.

Without waiting for an answer she gathered up my wet jeans and sweatshirt and hurried out of the room. "Why do you dress like a boy?" she called over her shoulder. "And why is your hair so short? Did you have head lice? Poor Zannah—how nasty! Loyal had lice, too, year before last, but a shaved head doesn't look quite so bad on a boy."

I followed her awkwardly downstairs, clutching the folds of my long skirt. "Nobody shaved my head," I said. "I don't call this short hair, anyway. Lots of the girls at school wear their hair much shorter. And we all wear jeans unless it's hot enough to wear cut-offs."

Utopia looked confused. Then her eyes opened wide. "School? Do you go to school, Zannah? Oh, the luck of some people! Tell me about it."

It isn't easy to describe a fifth-grade classroom to someone who doesn't seem to understand a word you say.

"Physical Ed?" she would repeat. "Who is that? What are markers? Why aren't girls allowed to enter the boys' room? Why does your school have separate rooms for boys and girls, instead of teaching them together?"

In the end I gave up and questioned her instead. We were sitting at the kitchen table. Utopia had draped my clothes over a rack in front of a big, wood-burning stove. While they steamed, filling the room with the stench of pond water, she spread honey on a slice of homemade bread.

"We used to have a schoolhouse, back when we were still part of the farm," she told me.

"Isn't this a farm?"

"No, silly, this is just the dairy. This house and the dairy building and the barn used to belong to an enormous farm— acres and acres of fields, as far as you could see."

I looked dubiously out the window at the thick woods on the far side of the meadow. "What happened to the rest of it?"

"It's still there," said Utopia. "At least, I presume it is. The point is, what happened to us."

"Well, what happened to you?" I asked impatiently.

"We were removed, of course. Before we were removed, there were seventeen children on the farm. Now there's just me and Loyal and the Noahs."

"The Noahs?" I repeated. "Who are they?"

"Oh, do stop interrupting!" Utopia cried. "I was telling you about our schoolhouse. There was one room for everybody, not separate rooms for boys and girls."

I was about to explain that I had been talking about restrooms, not classrooms, but Utopia went on dreamily.

"That's where I started to learn to read and figure. But when I was six Father had a falling out with that dreadful Mr. Rudge, and Mr. Rudge removed us. So Loyal had no schooling at all, and neither did Ham and Japheth. Shem can figure but he can't read, though he's turned thirteen. That's because he never went to class back then if he could avoid it, and now he says he's too old for schooling. Can't read at thirteen and too old to learn— can you credit it?"

Who was the dreadful Mr. Rudge? Who were Shem, Ham, and Japheth? Before I had a chance to ask, Loyal Graybeal burst through the door, followed by three other boys. Utopia stopped talking and set to work again with bread and honey. While she was slicing and spreading, Mr. Pratt slipped in and set a carton on the kitchen table. In it were the supplies I had seen in the back of the van. Except, unfortunately, for the peanut butter sandwich.

Utopia wiped her hands on a dishcloth and reached out eagerly. "Soap, molasses, candles, coffee, nails—" she counted. "Don't tell me you forgot the tobacco! And what about the book? The hairpins aren't here either. What happened, did you lose my list?"

I was shocked at her bossy tone, but Mr. Pratt just smiled. "Sorry, Utopia. The tobacco and the pins slipped my mind. I did look for a book, but there was nothing suitable."

Utopia frowned. "The book doesn't matter; it was only for me. But Father hasn't smoked his pipe since Monday. He'll be in a terrible mood when he learns there's no tobacco, and those candles won't help matters. Scarlet! And all those spangles—he'll say they're wicked! Weren't there any plain?"

The milkman looked rueful. "These were on sale. Left over from last Christmas, I gather. I'll bring the tobacco tomorrow, Utopia, and meanwhile if your father scolds, say it was my fault. Tobacco is bad for him anyway. You ought to tell him that."

An expression of doubt flashed over Utopia's face. "Bad for the body or bad for the soul?"

Mr. Pratt's mouth twitched. "I'm hardly an authority on souls. But the Surgeon General has determined that tobacco smoking is dangerous to the health."

"Then I won't tell him," Utopia said decidedly. "Father has no use for military men, and even if smoking were bad for the soul, it wouldn't be my place to tell him."

Picking up the empty carton, Mr. Pratt moved toward the kitchen door. "I'd better be on my way. Where *is* your father, by the way? And Mrs. Noah?"

"Out in the barn," Loyal answered in a voice muffled by bread and honey. "Our best milker is calving. Father says it's too soon to be safe. Mrs. Noah has been crying for five hours and thirty minutes, she's so upset. I counted."

"Then I won't add to the fuss," said Mr. Pratt. "Come along, Zannah McFee! There's bound to be someone missing you. Let's get you home before they call in the police."

I started to follow him, but Utopia blocked my way. "Oh, can't Zannah stay? She's the first girl I've seen since I was six years old! I haven't asked her half the questions I wanted, and her clothes aren't dry."

"I can't," I said, looking at my watch. "I'd love to, but I shouldn't have come in the first place. Patty—my mother, that is—will worry and besides, it's her birthday. I wanted to make her breakfast before I left for school."

Utopia paid no attention. She was staring wide-eyed at my wrist. "Can your bracelet tell the time?"

"Of course," I said. "It's a watch."

She touched it apprehensively. "But it has no hands or face—how does it work?"

At first I thought she was making fun of me. "It's a digital watch, silly. I don't know how it works. I'm surprised it works at all, as a matter of fact. It isn't supposed to be waterproof."

Then I realized that she was quite serious, and I laughed. It isn't every day that you meet someone who has never seen a digital watch. "Here, you can borrow it," I said, slipping it off my wrist. "I'll get it when I bring back your clothes. I only hope it goes on working, after that dip in the pond."

Utopia's eyes shone. "Then we'll trade, until you come again."

She reached up, fumbled at her neck, and held out a little gold locket on a chain. "Come back soon, Zannah," she whispered. "Come back very soon!"

I rode home on the driver's bench, behind the mare. Mr. Pratt was silent at first. He seemed to be thinking hard. That was fine with me, because I had thinking of my own to do. Who were those people with all the weird names? I liked them, but some of the things they said were just plain crazy. Like Utopia not knowing what a zipper was, and all that talk about being removed. Everyone at the dairy sounded a little nutty, including the weepy Mrs. Noah and Utopia's father who thought red candles were wicked.

"Are those people in their right minds?" I asked. "I mean, that wasn't some kind of home for the mentally disturbed or something, was it?"

Mr. Pratt shook his head impatiently. "Don't talk now," he said. "This is the tricky part. If I can just get you out of these woods, everything will be hunky-dory."

We trotted along through the trees, following a track that didn't look much used. When we finally came out on a paved road, the milkman's face brightened, and he turned to smile triumphantly at me.

"Hey, we're back in Burleith!" I cried. "That dairy must have been in Archbold Glover Park. I never knew people actually lived in Glover Park. I thought it was nothing but trees."

Mr. Pratt looked a little uncomfortable. "Well—life is full of surprises."

"Oh, I get it!" I said suddenly. "It's one of those places that schools go to on field trips. 'Life on a Dairy Farm: Hands-on Experience for City Kids.' Right?"

"Not exactly," said Mr. Pratt. He veered to the side of the road to let a car go by. "You're nearly home now, Zannah McFee, and you've been asking all the questions. Let's have *your* story."

I told him everything, from Patty's heart's desire to the moment the mare started moving with me still inside the van. "And I'm truly sorry about your sandwich," I said at last, "but if you stop by my house I'll run inside and make you another."

He smiled. "You're welcome to the sandwich. That's not what bothers me. The question is, how did you get to the dairy?"

"In your van, like I told you," I said. "Do you think you could take me back there sometime? I have to give Utopia her locket and these clothes, and my jeans and sweatshirt are still drying in her kitchen."

Mr. Pratt stopped smiling and rubbed his chin. "Will it work a second time, that's the question. It never worked before. Chances are I can't get you there."

He sounded as nutty as the rest of them, but at least he wasn't angry. In fact he reached behind the seat and pulled out a quart of milk. It didn't look like supermarket milk; it was in a bottle, not a carton, and had about an inch of yellow cream on top. Still, it was better than nothing, especially since he wouldn't let me pay for it. I thanked him, and thanked him again when he handed me a morning paper.

"I really shouldn't take your paper though," I said. "I can buy one on my way back from school."

"You won't find this edition," said Mr. Pratt. "Take it and welcome, and tell your mother 'happy birthday.' I'd tell her myself, but I'm late to work."

"Isn't this your work?" I asked.

Mr. Pratt threw back his head and laughed. "That depends on how you look at it. It's work all right, but it doesn't pay the rent."

I felt dizzy with confusion. Nothing made sense that morning. "Then why do you do it?"

"If I didn't, who would?" he asked. "Get ready to jump down now. You're home."

When the van drew up outside my house, Patty was on the front steps with a worried face. She stared at the mare, and at the van, and at me in my long brown dress. Then she went limp, as if every bone in her body had turned to jelly.

Mr. Pratt took one look and hurried over to reassure her. He apparently changed his mind about being late for work because in the middle of his chat with Patty he looked up and said, "What about that sandwich, Zannah? Brown bread, please, and plenty of jelly."

By the time I came out with the sandwich, Patty had perked up and the color was back in her cheeks. She waved good-bye to Mr. Pratt and sent me into the house to change. "Wherever did you get that dress?" she asked.

"I borrowed it from a girl I met. Her brother fell into the pond, and—"

"Oh, never mind," said Patty. "You can tell me this afternoon. Hurry now, or we'll both be late for school."

On my way upstairs to get another pair of jeans, I shouted,
"Your heart's desire is on the kitchen counter, Patty!"

A few minutes later I found Patty staring at the paper in
amazement. "Where on earth did you get it?" she asked. "What
a marvelous birthday present! You're a darling, Zannah—it must
have cost you a fortune!"

I'm used to having a zany mother, but this was the limit. It
wasn't at all unusual for her to send me for the morning paper,
and the most she had ever said before was "Thanks."

"I got it for free," I told her quietly. "Not that I couldn't
spare twenty-five cents."

Then I took a casual look at the front page and nearly fainted.
The date at the top was October, 1881.

CHAPTER 2

PATTY AND I usually came home together in the afternoon. She might be a little late due to figuring out which boots went with which Tiny, but most days when I reached St. Michael's Church, she was waiting on the steps. On the afternoon of her birthday, I didn't go by the church at all, however. As soon as school let out, I started uphill toward the market. Besides the roses I needed a cake mix and some frosting.

I ran as hard as I could, hoping for once that Patty would have trouble with boots again, or that Lafayette, her assistant, would have lost an earring. Lafayette was nice, and she was really popular with the Tinies, but she was every bit as absent-minded as Patty, and the last time she lost an earring it held Patty up for a whole hour. The combined niceness and absent-mindedness of Lafayette and Patty was my biggest worry in life. They were all give and no take, and how can people like that hope to get rich and safe and happy?

I worried about them while I shopped, and hurried home, and threw the mix together. And I was in luck: the cake was baked and iced by the time Patty came home. But from the look on her face I could tell it wasn't cake she needed so much as a drink. Luckily I had one ready.

"Happy birthday to you!" I sang as she walked in the door. "You live in a zoo! You look like a monkey—"

Patty smiled in spite of herself. "Roses? A cake? Oh, Zannah, you're spoiling me!"

"My pleasure," I told her. "Have some bubbly?"

I was proud of the champagne, which I had wheedled out of one of Patty's boyfriends. It was nesting in a bucket of ice now, restaurant style.

Patty's face grew downright cheerful as she poured champagne into two glasses, diluting mine with ginger ale. "Where did this come from? Don't tell me you passed for eighteen!"

"Danny Friedman got it for me. He says 'happy birthday,' by the way. He says if I'd asked him earlier, he would have enclosed a card."

Patty's face fell again. "Oh, Zannah, don't tell me you *asked* Danny to give me a bottle of champagne!"

"I didn't exactly ask," I explained. "I sort of hinted. After all, what are boyfriends for?"

"But he isn't my boyfriend," said Patty. "He's just the ordinary sort of friend."

That was news to me. "Since when?" I asked suspiciously.

"Officially as of a week from tomorrow," said Patty. "He's getting married."

I sighed and set down my glass. "Not to you, I take it."

"No, not to me," said Patty. "Why don't you give up, Zannah? I appreciate your efforts, but if I ever get married again, I can find my own husband."

I wasn't too sure about that, but I had the tact to change the subject. "What went wrong today? Why were you so late getting home?"

"It's Friday," Patty moaned. "The only good thing about Friday is it's the end of the week. I bet there hasn't been a crisis in the history of the playgroup that didn't happen on a Friday."

"Except all the ones that happened on Monday, Tuesday,

Wednesday, and Thursday," I told her. "Come on, share your troubles."

Patty had had enough champagne to discuss her troubles with a sense of humor, and there's no doubt that it was funny.

One of the Tinies was supposed to go home and play with one of the other Tinies after school. Nothing unusual about that, except that Patty got the kids mixed up. She mixed their raincoats up first, actually, and then sent the wrong Tiny home with his friend's father. The father didn't know one Tiny from another and the children, who were perfectly happy with the new arrangement, didn't bother to complain. As for the Tiny who got left behind, he was picked up by a baby-sitter who had never met her charge, and taken home to the wrong house.

"But that's ridiculous!" I spluttered. "How could that kid go off with a strange sitter? And when the sitter asked for him, how come you gave her the wrong Tiny? I know, don't tell me—you got them mixed up. But even so, when the kid came to the wrong house he must have said something."

Patty shrugged and giggled. "Apparently not. Apparently he was tickled pink to have all those new toys to play with. So nothing happened until his mother came home. The woman who *thought* she was his mother, that is. Anyway, you know what I mean."

"I do, but I bet nobody else would," I said. "How could you be so absentminded? I bet everyone was furious!"

"They were," said Patty. "It took a long time to straighten out, too. For a while I couldn't remember whose house—"

"Okay, okay, don't tell me. I can imagine," I said.

Patty poured herself another glass of champagne and gave me an impish glance. "Oh, Zannah—I wish you could have seen their faces!"

I had a brief struggle, trying to keep my dignity. Then we both burst out laughing.

"Well, eat, drink, and be merry," I said. "Oh, and I almost forgot your present!"

"Another present?" said Patty. "I thought my present was that century-old *Washington Post*."

"I got that for free," I told her. "This is something I saved up for. It's going to change your life."

Patty groaned. "Oh, Zannah—not another man?"

The champagne was definitely going to her head. "I don't pay your boyfriends," I informed her. "I have more subtle ways of recruiting them. Besides, all they have to do is see you, and they're hooked. You're pretty good-looking for thirty-one, you know."

Patty laughed and opened her present. "How sweet! What is it?"

"It's a calculator," I said. "Here, I'll show you how to use it."

I asked Patty for a sample problem and she came up with a real teaser. One of the Tinies had been absent for two weeks. Patty had been soft enough to refund his tuition, but the parents had agreed to pay the part that went to Lafayette, and they owed some money for art supplies, too. It was fairly complicated, but I worked it out in no time flat and showed Patty the final result.

"See? You refunded them more than they paid you in the first place. If they were honest, they'd give it back."

Patty said that come to think of it, the parents had given her an envelope the other day, but she had forgotten to open it. After hunting for a few minutes she found it in her purse, inside a half-empty bag of potato chips. Sure enough, it contained a greasy check for $41.50.

"Oh, for heaven's sake!" I said. "You're hopeless! Why doesn't Lafayette help you with some of the paperwork?"

"She helps a lot," said Patty. "It's just she's awfully slow. She gets slower every day. I think it's because she's been putting on weight recently. I'm trying to convince her to sign up with Weight Watchers."

"If she's that fat she can't be getting enough exercise," I said ruthlessly. "I don't see *you* putting on any weight. Those kids are wearing you to a frazzle! Why don't you give it up and go back to your job at the hospital?"

Patty was a registered nurse, or had been up until a few years before. I considered it much more interesting work than running after a bunch of preschoolers and it paid better, too, but Patty refused to see it from my point of view.

"Oh, Zannah! Don't get started on that track again," she said. "We hardly saw each other back then, remember? At least now we keep the same hours."

I offered to put in some time at Saint Michael's and pull the Tiny Fingers Preschool Playgroup together for Patty, but she said it was more important to work at my own education.

That reminded me of Utopia and all the other children who didn't have to go to school but wished they could, except for Shem. I told Patty about the dairy, and she was as intrigued as I was.

"A model farm in Glover Park? I've never heard of it. What an adventure! I'm not too happy about your hitching a ride in that van, though."

"It was an accident," I said. "Besides, you have to admit Mr. Pratt is a nice guy. After all, you talked to him."

Patty admitted that Mr. Pratt was a nice guy, but she still felt obliged to repeat her lecture on accepting rides from strange men.

"I wasn't planning on accepting a ride," I reminded her. "All I wanted was a bottle of milk. But is it okay if he takes me back so I can give Utopia her clothes and her locket? She has my sweatshirt and jeans. They were sopping."

Patty took a close look at the locket. "What a darling, old-fashioned little thing! It looks like an heirloom. I'm surprised her mother let you take it."

"Her mother wasn't there," I explained. "Anyway, Utopia has my watch, so it's sort of a guarantee. We traded. If I didn't bring her locket back it would be a what-do-you-call-it, a breach of faith."

Patty sighed. "You win, sweetheart. You can go back, but on one condition: I'm taking you there."

We looked up the Hunky-Dory Dairy in the phone book, but it wasn't listed. Then we looked up dairies in the yellow pages. None of the places sounded right, and it wasn't mentioned in any of our guidebooks either. That evening we drove around Burleith for half an hour searching for the track into Archbold Glover Park, but we couldn't find it, so we went home and polished off the birthday cake before going to bed.

Generally Patty and I sleep late on Saturdays because there's no school for either of us, but the next morning we got up early and walked to the spot where the mare had been standing in the rain. There she was again, with her nose in a feedbag. Mr. Pratt was just running down the steps of a town house, an empty bottle in each hand.

"Good morning!" he called. "You're up early. Need some milk? I'd be glad to put you on my route."

Patty said she would adore it, but what we really came for was directions to the dairy so she could drive me over with the clothes.

Mr. Pratt took off his cap and scratched his head thoughtfully. He looked a little embarrassed. "It's a dirt track, you know," he said at last. "A car wouldn't make it."

Patty shrugged. "We'll walk, then. Glover Park isn't all that big. If you'll just tell us how—"

He looked more embarrassed than ever. "It's kind of tricky. I tell you what: why doesn't she come with me in the van, like yesterday?"

I could tell Patty wasn't going to allow that. She kept looking from me to Mr. Pratt and back to me again. But then she surprised me by breaking into a grin that made her look twelve years old.

"Can I come, too?"

"I'd be delighted!" said Mr. Pratt. "This is the last house on my route. We can set off now, if that's all right with you. I'd be interested to see if this works for you as well as for your daughter."

Patty looked bewildered as he helped her up to the seat, unhooked the feedbag, and started the mare with a little flick of the reins. I was sitting close enough to hear him muttering, "Will it work again, that's the question—will it work a second time?"

Suddenly I remembered that Utopia's clothes were still up in my room. Mr. Pratt turned the van onto our street and stopped outside our house for the time it took me to run in and get them.

"You wouldn't happen to have a packet of hairpins while you're at it, would you?" he asked.

I laughed. "Are you crazy? Patty might have some, though. She used to have long hair."

"Second drawer from the top, left-hand side," said Patty.

I started up our front walk, wondering what it takes to make a mind like Patty's. She sends a Tiny home to the wrong house and then can't remember which house she sent him to, but she can put her finger on a hairpin that she hasn't used for three years.

"Oh, and Zannah!" Mr. Pratt called after me. "How about lending Utopia a book? She wants fiction, but it has to be *proper* fiction, if you know what I mean."

"No, I *don't* know," I said, coming back to the van. "What's proper fiction? No sex?"

"Worse than that," said Mr. Pratt. "It'll have to be religious, or at least very moralizing, or her father won't let her read it."

"Oh, poor Utopia!" I said. "Nancy Drew won't qualify, I take it?"

Mr. Pratt shook his head. "Definitely not."

"Or the Black Stallion?"

"I'm afraid not," he said apologetically. "You see, her father—"

"I know," I interrupted. "I've got just the thing."

I ran into the house and came back with the hairpins and a paperback copy of *The Secret Garden*. Mr. Pratt looked pleased, but to my surprise he flipped it open, frowned, and tore out the page with all the little print about things like copyright.

"Hey, what are you doing?" I protested.

"Sorry, Zannah," he said, "but I don't want anyone to get upset. Nineteen-eleven, you know. You don't mind, do you?"

All I minded was that such a nice man was a raving lunatic, so I kept my mouth shut and enjoyed the ride to the Hunky-Dory Dairy.

Patty was enjoying herself, too, but I noticed that she looked more and more perplexed, as if she were trying to work out a problem. I thought at first that it was something to do with the Tiny Fingers Playgroup, but when the van crossed 42nd Street and entered the dirt track into the woods, I knew it was our route that bothered her.

It was obvious that something bothered Mr. Pratt, as well. His face went through all sorts of contortions as we entered the woods. It was almost as if he didn't really dare go ahead. But once we were among the trees he gave a sigh of relief and looked positively cheerful.

When we pulled up in front of the farmhouse, the children

were nowhere to be seen, but we were met at the kitchen door by two grown-ups. Mr. Pratt turned quickly, grabbed my shoulder, and whispered, "That's Hector Graybeal. Keep the book in your pocket, Zannah, until further notice."

The first thought that came into my head was that Hector Graybeal was the handsomest man I had ever seen outside my history book. He looked just like Abraham Lincoln, only without the wart on his cheek.

As for the woman, she was pretty, but she was a mess. Her red-golden curls were screwed up on top of her head where she had tried unsuccessfully to fasten them with a piece of dirty string. There was something like jam on her nose, and her white apron was splattered with more of the same. She wore a long, brown dress just like Utopia's. Her feet were bare, too, and looked as if she hadn't bothered to wash them lately.

The woman started to smile but stopped again, after a timid glance at Hector Graybeal. I smiled back and held out Patty's hairpins. "You must be Mrs. Graybeal, Utopia's mother," I said. "I guess these are for you."

Hector Graybeal scowled. "What's this? Hairpins? More frills and farfellews? Woman, thy name is gaudery!"

"Oh, no, it isn't!" the woman squeaked. "And it isn't Graybeal either. My name is Marigold Rudge. Poor Utopia's mama is with the angels."

With the angels? Meaning dead? I was sorry for Utopia, but I have to admit I was also glad because a glorious idea occurred to me. What if Patty fell in love with Hector Graybeal? He hadn't been very pleasant so far, but surely his bark was worse than his bite, and who could resist a man who looked like President Lincoln?

"Oh, Mr. Graybeal," I said. "I'm so happy to meet you! I'm Zannah McFee—did Utopia tell you about me? And this is Patty, my mother."

Hector Graybeal ignored me and stared at Patty with a scandalized face. "Patty? Short for Patience, I presume."

Patty shook her head. "No. I was christened 'Patty.' "

"Christened!" he repeated, raising his bushy eyebrows. " 'Patty' is hardly a Christian name. And why, may I ask, are you masquerading as a man?" His eyes dropped to Patty's jeans and then looked quickly away. "A woman in trousers is an abomination in the eyes of the Lord!"

As Hector Graybeal turned his back and strode into the house, Patty blushed—a thing I had never known her to do before. Marigold Rudge blushed, too, in sympathy. As for Mr. Pratt, he made a solemn face, but his blue eyes twinkled.

"Holy smoke!" he said. "My fault, I should have thought of it. Wait in the kitchen with Mrs. Noah, Patty. I'll see if I can smooth things over."

Marigold Rudge looked so shy after he left that I felt sorry for her. "Why does he call you Mrs. Noah if your name is Rudge?" I asked, by way of conversation.

"Mr. Pratt is fond of joking," she explained. "My boys are named Shem, Ham, and Japheth, after Noah's children in the ark."

I remembered yesterday's conversation. "Oh, yes, Utopia told me. I haven't met them yet. Then is your husband's name Noah Rudge?"

At the mention of her husband, Mrs. Noah turned pale. "I don't know whether I have a husband or not," she whispered. "I lost him five years ago. That is, he lost me—if you can speak of losing when it was deliberate casting away. Oh, dear, I don't know what's to become of me!"

She dabbed at her eyes with a corner of her apron, spreading the jam from her nose to her cheek so that she looked like a lopsided clown.

I was about to beg for details when the youngest Noah popped

"And why, may I ask, are you masquerading as a man?"

his head around the door and beckoned. "Quick, Zannah!" he hissed. "Utopia needs help. Loyal forgot to latch the henhouse door, and the chickens are in the dairy."

Mrs. Noah moaned and collapsed on a chair, so I gathered that it was a real emergency. True enough, the dairy was swarming with chickens, all in a panic and squawking their heads off. The fact that Loyal and the older Noahs were chasing them around the milk cans didn't help one bit.

Only Utopia remained calm. "Go away, Loyal—you're doing more harm than good! Ham and Japheth, you go with him. Or wait—all three of you stand just outside the door and Zannah and I will hand out the chickens one by one. Help us, Shem! Don't just stand there laughing like the great lout you are. Or do you intend to let the girls do all the work?"

Shem stopped laughing and eyed me with suspicion. "That's no girl," he grumbled. "If that's a girl, where are her skirts?"

I pushed him aside impatiently and started lunging at the chickens. "This is a farm, not a birthday party. What's wrong with you people? Haven't you ever seen a pair of jeans before?"

I wasn't used to chickens and I didn't much like the way they pecked at my ankles, but I was as quick as Shem at catching them. Utopia kept tripping in her long, brown dress.

"Why on earth you don't wear jeans yourself I can't imagine," I told her when the birds were safely locked away and we were inspecting the dairy for the last few telltale feathers.

Utopia didn't look as shocked as she might have the day before. "I wouldn't mind, but Father would be angry. Worse than angry. It would be like—like the wrath of God! He would say I was an abomination—"

"In the face of the Lord," I finished. "I know. He just called my mother one."

Utopia giggled. "Is your mother here? In britches? I wish I could have seen Father's face. But I'll tell you a secret, if you promise not to repeat it to a single soul. Only Loyal saw me, but I made him swear a solemn vow."

I swore a solemn vow. "Cut my throat and hope to die," I added for good measure. "What is it? What did Loyal see you do?"

Utopia's eyes sparkled and her voice fell to a whisper. "I wore them, while Father and the boys were milking."

"You wore what?" I asked. "My jeans?"

Utopia nodded excitedly. "They're lovely," she said. "You're so lucky, Zannah!"

I was dying to find out more about this crazy place where no one had ever seen jeans or digital watches, but I was concerned about Patty, alone in the kitchen with Mrs. Noah. I needn't have worried, though. When I went back, Patty was wearing the apron, which was as long and full as a dress. Both women were gossiping like old friends, and Patty was doing something fancy with the hairpins and Mrs. Noah's hair.

"What do you think, Zannah?" she asked. "Doesn't Marigold look gorgeous with a French twist?"

"Gorgeous!" I agreed. "But what will Mr. Graybeal say?"

Mrs. Noah turned pale, but Patty laughed. "Why should he say anything at all? She's not his wife."

I was glad she had registered the fact; it was a step on the way to romance. And truly, I thought Patty better suited than Mrs. Noah to a man with a mind of his own and a sharp temper. Patty got mixed up, but she was no coward.

"It needs another pin there at the top," I said.

But before I had time to show her where, Mr. Pratt came back into the kitchen, followed by Hector Graybeal, who was beaming.

"My poor woman!" said Mr. Graybeal, taking Patty's hand in his and squeezing it. "Why did you not tell me of your shocking plight? I would be the first to sympathize."

Patty looked at her hand as if it belonged to someone else. Then she looked helplessly at Mr. Pratt.

"Oh, please don't feel shy! Please don't blush!" said Mr. Graybeal, although this time I didn't notice Patty blushing. "How humiliating for a lonely widow to be forced to such extremes, and how I approve of your adopting this disguise!"

Patty looked more confused than ever. "Disguise?"

"Yes, my dear. Only dressed as a man could you escape such wicked overtures. But you are safe with us. Here you may resume your womanly garb and live in peace and virtue. Welcome, Patience!"

Was he proposing marriage? If so, it was quicker than any courtship I had ever dreamed of. In fact I was disappointed; where was the romance?

From the way Patty blinked and swallowed I could tell she was trying to keep a straight face. Pulling her hand away quietly, she gave Mr. Pratt a dirty look. "That's very kind of you, Mr. Graybeal, but I think I'm out of danger now, and much as I appreciate your offer, I'm afraid I can't stay. I'm a teacher of sorts, you see. I'm in charge of twelve children all week long, and I can't let them down."

This information drove Hector Graybeal into a state of frenzy. "A schoolteacher?" he cried. "How fortunate! The good Lord must have sent you to us. The children here are sorely in need of education. Stay, Patience! We will offer you protection in return for your services."

I bit my knuckles to keep from giggling. Hector Graybeal would be shocked if he knew how little Patty needed his protection. She had been single for eleven years and was an expert at telling a man where to get off if she didn't feel like getting too friendly with him. On the other hand, teaching five children at the dairy would be a lot easier on her than teaching a dozen in the basement of Saint Michael's Church.

That last thought decided me; I would give Hector Graybeal my full support. "She's a nurse, too," I informed him sweetly. "If anyone got sick, she'd know just what to do."

When he heard that, Hector Graybeal began to sound less preachy and more as if he really meant it, but Patty didn't give in. She insisted not only on going home, but on going home immediately. I barely had time to take Utopia aside and slip her *The Secret Garden* before we were trotting off toward the woods behind the dapple-gray mare.

"You are a brave woman, Patience!" Hector Graybeal called after us. "May God protect you! When you need a home, you will find one here!"

Patty waited until we were back on 42nd Street before turning to Mr. Pratt. "All right, wise guy," she said coldly. "I don't know what you told that maniac, but I can guess. Now tell *me* something."

"Glad to," said Mr. Pratt. "Tell you what?"

"What does it mean?" Patty demanded. "There's no dairy farm in Archbold Glover Park. There's no open space in there at all—you know as well as I do. And for sure there's no track leading off 42nd Street. We drove right by there yesterday, and I remember."

"I see," said Mr. Pratt. "You're confused geographically, so to speak."

"You're damn right I am!" said Patty. "Anyone in his right mind would be. But that's not all. Those people are unreal—they can't be true. Why, they could be right out of another century!"

After a moment, Mr. Pratt sighed. "That's the problem," he said. "They are."

CHAPTER 3

I FELT SORRY for Mr. Pratt. When anyone tries to put something over on Patty she loses her temper in a big way unless it's hysterically funny, which this wasn't. But on the contrary, instead of being angry, Patty seemed relieved.

"So that's it!" she said. "I was beginning to wonder whether I was dreaming or if I had just lost what was left of my mind. Now, tell me how you came to find them."

Mr. Pratt slowed the mare down to a walk. "It happened two years ago," he began. "I was running on the towpath with a girlfriend of mine, down by the canal. She and I used to meet after work and run six miles round-trip. To keep in shape, you know."

Patty made a noncommittal noise; she keeps in shape, but she's never been one to run for the sake of running.

"This particular day, we did our three miles out and were on our way back when I saw a big splash and heard a child screaming. It was Loyal Graybeal and young Ham, the middle Noah. They'd been fishing and Loyal fell in, of course. You can count on Loyal to fall in whenever there's something bigger than a thimble to fall into. The two of them were only six years old back then, and neither of them could swim. Loyal still can't, as Zannah knows. So I jumped in and pulled him out by his suspenders, and gave him the scolding he deserved."

"What about your friend?" I asked.

"That's when I realized things weren't all they seemed," said Mr. Pratt. "She had fallen a bit behind by then. When she caught up and saw me soaking wet, giving a piece of my mind to thin air, she panicked and took off."

"Thin air?" I repeated. "You mean she couldn't see Loyal?"

"You guessed it," said Mr. Pratt. "She couldn't see either of them. She thought I was playing a joke on her and she wasn't having any of it, so she ran on home and refused to speak to me for ten days.

"I didn't chase after her to explain because I wanted to take those children back where they belonged, before Loyal succeeded in drowning himself. They had run up the path into the woods where Glover Park meets the canal. I followed right after them and after a while the woods opened up, though I'd run on that path at least a dozen times and knew as well as anyone that there's nothing there but trees. But this time I saw a meadow, and a bunch of cows, and the dairy. I met the whole crew that day: Hector and his kids, and Marigold and hers. They were a sorry bunch if I ever saw one."

"Why?" I asked. "They don't look a bit sorry now, except maybe Mrs. Noah."

"They'd met up with hard times," Mr. Pratt explained. "It seems they were part of an experimental community, a little like a commune nowadays. Back in the nineteenth century there were quite a few places like that, where families got together away from the sin or the injustice of the outside world. They designed their own little social system and tried to be self-sufficient. To make it on their own, you know.

"The community that the Graybeals had joined was run by a man named Rudge—a preacher who had had a falling out with his church over what they called 'unorthodox behavior.' I gather that meant black magic. He and his followers bought some land across the Potomac River in Virginia, and they did fine for a while. They built their own chapel and their schoolhouse and the dairy, of course, and they planted all the usual crops. They made their own soap and candles, and put up preserves for winter. They wove their own cloth and baked their own bread and didn't lack for anything but salt, and kerosene, and coffee, and suchlike. They got those by trading their surplus, back in town."

"It sounds like fun!" I said.

"It sounds like awfully hard work," said Patty.

"There's the snag," said Mr. Pratt. "It wasn't. That's what troubled Graybeal. He's no fool, and he began to notice things. The cows were milking themselves, for instance. I mean, they stood still, but the milk squirted into the pails with no one there to do it. The cloth wove itself and the bread kneaded itself, and most of the crops came up overnight, just like Jack's beanstalk. No one raised a finger."

"How lovely!" said Patty with a sigh.

"You may think so," said Mr. Pratt, "but it was too much for Hector Graybeal. Running the dairy was his job, and he didn't like what was happening to his cows. Graybeal is straight as they come—took religion a lot more seriously than Rudge, and still does. He wanted no dealings with witchcraft, and he threatened to bring in the law and have the man locked up. Not that the law would have taken the business seriously, if you ask me, but Rudge wasn't taking any risks, so apparently he snapped his fingers and wished the dairy off to where Graybeal would never be a nuisance to anyone again."

"That's a fairy tale," I said crossly. "People just can't do that."

Mr. Pratt shrugged. "It worked, though. The magic did, that is. The rest was a disaster. In the first place, he didn't know that his wife was in the dairy, making cheese. His boys, Shem and

Ham and Japheth, were in the kitchen with the Graybeal kids. So his own family got magicked away with the rest of them, over the river and into another century. Not that Mrs. Noah seemed to mind. She didn't hold with Rudge's ways any more than Graybeal did, and she was always a little afraid of him."

"Then why was it a disaster?" I asked.

"Because they weren't self-sufficient any longer. They couldn't make it on their own. Or just barely, at any rate. They had the cows, and the dairy, and a few chickens, and that was all.

"They made a valiant go at it. Graybeal planted some crops. Mrs. Noah took over the kitchen and put up a few preserves. Still, neither of them was any hand at carpentry, or weaving, or even soap and candles, to say nothing of teaching the children. Things began to fall apart. When I met the two families they'd been at it for close to three years and were about to give up, except there was no place else they could go to. They can't get out."

"What about Mrs. Graybeal?" I asked. "Did she get left behind?"

"There was no Mrs. Graybeal," said the milkman. "Not at that point, at least. She died of the measles, believe it or not, when Loyal was a baby. I tell you, they were a sorry lot. Lovable, too, in their way, so I did what I could to help. It was my idea to start the milk route in Burleith. They had plenty of milk and butter, and once Utopia was old enough to take them over, the hens began laying better. They had the mare and an old van. I told them if they'd let me sell their surplus, I could bring back some of the extras they needed and things would be hunky-dory. That's why the name. Shem gave the van a new coat of paint, and Utopia did the lettering: 'Hunky-Dory Dairy: Milk, Butter, and Eggs.'

"We got quite a little business going. Our products are pop-ular in this neighborhood; they look old-fashioned, so people think they're healthier than the supermarket stuff. It's time-consuming, though. Often as not I'm late to work in the morning."

"What's your work?" asked Patty.

"Office job," said Mr. Pratt. "I won't go into it; it would bore you to tears. Bores me, too. One of these days I'll have to look for something else, but I'm too busy to do anything about it, what with dropping all those orders off, six days a week."

"Don't you work on Sundays?" I asked.

"You bet your life I don't," said Mr. Pratt. "On Sundays, Graybeal preaches. Fire and brimstone, morning to night. I stay away. It drives the rest of the crew out of their minds, poor things, but they can't get away from it. I guess Graybeal's theory is the harder he preaches, the less chance there is of witchcraft taking over his dairy a second time."

"Maybe Utopia could come over to my house some Sunday," I suggested. "*All* the kids could. You wouldn't mind, would you, Patty?"

"It wouldn't work," Mr. Pratt said without giving Patty the time to answer. "I tried it. Get one of those kids in the van and the mare won't leave the woods. They can't walk out, either. Something holds them back when they get close to civilization. It's all part of Rudge's magic. The farthest afield any of them has been is the canal, down where the boys like to fish. Even there, no one can see them. Rudge said they were never to be a nuisance again, remember?"

"But *you* saw them," I corrected him. "And now Patty and I can see them too."

"That's what surprised me yesterday," said Mr. Pratt. "Two years ago I tried to bring someone in to meet them. My girlfriend, as a matter of fact. Remember how it was ten days before she'd speak to me? Well, when she did I told her the whole story and she agreed to come and see. But when we got to the track in the park it wasn't there. The woods closed up around it, and there was no way to drive in. We tried walking in, but we couldn't find the dairy. She never forgave me. It was the end of a beautiful friendship."

"If I were you I'd be glad," I said. "She doesn't sound very nice. But if she couldn't get in, why does it work for you and me and Patty?"

"Beats me," said Mr. Pratt.

Patty smiled. "Perhaps it's because to the three of us they're not a nuisance."

Mr. Pratt had dropped the reins while he told his story, but the mare turned onto our street instinctively and stopped in front of our house. "Here we are," said Mr. Pratt. "How are you doing for milk?" He pulled a quart bottle from the carrier and handed it to Patty.

"Hey, wait a minute!" I said. "I'm not sure how I feel about drinking hundred-year-old milk."

"Think about it over the weekend," Mr. Pratt advised me. "I'll stop by for the empties on Monday, and you can tell me if you want to be one of my regulars."

"Oh, we do!" Patty said happily. "I can tell you right away, we do!"

When we came downstairs on Monday morning, the milk was already standing outside the front door, with a pound of butter and a dozen eggs. Mr. Pratt had come and gone.

"Damn!" said Patty. "I forgot to put out the empties. Put them out now, will you, Zannah? Maybe he'll stop by again later."

It turned out she had more to worry over than milk that morning. It was Columbus Day, and schools were closed. Normally Patty and I would have taken a picnic to the river or gone to a museum. We might even have spent the whole day at the

Hunky-Dory Dairy, for that matter, but luck was against us. Patty had forgotten Columbus Day, and the Tinies' delighted parents were careful not to remind her.

"Oh, well," I said when she broke the news. "Every cloud has a silver lining. I can come and help you out for once."

It was good I did. Lafayette had her head screwed on right; she knew perfectly well it was Columbus Day, and she never showed up. Two of the Tinies didn't show up either. They were the ones Patty had sent home to the wrong houses, and we found out later that their parents had switched them to another school. But that still left ten.

The Tiny Fingers Preschool Playgroup was a new experience for me. I knew all about it, of course; Patty gave me a blow-by-blow account every day at supper. But I had never actually stuck around and watched how it worked.

All the other preschools I've ever heard of have their day mapped out. There's singing time, story time, show-and-tell time, and snack time. In a pinch, the teacher can always take the whole class to the bathroom and kill half an hour getting their clothes buttoned up again. But not Patty. She reminded me of a kid in my class who did an act in the school talent show, spinning twenty tops at once. When he got the twentieth top spinning, he had to scoot around to give the first another twist and start all over again. Patty was just like that, running from one Tiny to the next. By the time she had the last one settled down with a puzzle, she was rushing back to scoop the Play-Doh out of the first one's mouth. Even when they needed the bathroom, she took them one by one.

"This is crazy!" I said. "Why don't you just read them all a story?"

"That's not done anymore," said Patty. "The idea nowadays is small-group activities."

"That's just a polite term for chaos," I told her. "Give yourself a break! I'll take half of them outside to play 'Simon Says,' and you can play 'Billy Goats Gruff' with the other five."

Patty looked doubtful. "There are only three billy goats and one troll. Somebody is going to feel left out."

I groaned. "Try having two trolls. Or if you'd rather, you can take the 'Simon Says' group."

Patty said she'd rather stay inside, so I took my Tinies out and we did just fine, but when we came back in again I realized that chaos or not, I should never have left Patty alone.

"What happened?" I asked when I found her, pale and frazzled, in the middle of an empty room. "Where did they go?"

"The bathroom," said Patty. "The biggest billy goat gruff had to pee, so the other two followed him, and the trolls went roaring along behind."

"So what's wrong with that?" I asked.

"They locked themselves in," Patty explained. "I've been calling and calling, but I can't get a sound out of them. Do you think there could be toxic fumes?"

"No such luck," I said. "I've been in that bathroom, and it's no worse than most. Don't worry, I'll get them out for you."

I marched over to the bathroom door, turned my back to it, and announced in a loud voice, "Okay, snack time! I've got ten cupcakes here, but I only see five kids. I guess that makes two apiece."

I was wrong to turn my back to the door because it flew open before I had time to get away. My method was painful, but effective. Patty was still upset, though. She pointed out that Monday's snack was graham crackers, not cupcakes. The market was only a few blocks away, so I offered to go buy cupcakes, although it would have served all those trolls and billy goats right if I didn't.

"Oh, and Zannah!" Patty called after me. "Buy some macaroni, too. We're making macaroni necklaces this afternoon, and I'm afraid I didn't bring enough."

I have to admit that I took my time at the market. I met a friend there, and we put a lot of quarters in the video machines. By the time I got back to Saint Michael's Church the Tinies had finished their graham crackers and were already making macaroni necklaces. They were a real mess.

"What's all that purple stuff in their hair?" I asked.

"Paint," said Patty.

"Good grief!" I said. "Don't you know you have to let the necklaces dry before the kids put them on? Their parents are going to have a fit! Purple is the hardest color to get off, too. Better take it away and give them yellow instead."

"The purple is all gone," croaked Patty.

She sounded so strange that I ran up and peered into her eyes. "What's up? You look terrible! Do you feel sick or something?"

"It's not me," said Patty. "It's Zippo. He drank the purple paint."

My heart sank, but I didn't panic. "So what? The stuff is nontoxic, isn't it? Show me the jar."

Patty found the empty jar and I read the label. " 'Nontoxic, as defined in the Federal Hazardous Substances Act.' See? Nothing to worry about."

Patty was not reassured. "It'll be the end of me, I tell you, Zannah. Someone is sure to notice. All that color has to come out again, doesn't it? I suppose I'd better warn the parents. They'll probably take the kid out of the playgroup."

"Never mind. You don't want a kid who drinks up all your paint anyway," I said. "Which one is Zippo?"

Patty looked around with a dazed expression on her face and then brightened. "We don't have a Zippo, actually. Unless it's someone's nickname."

"Oh, for heaven's sake! If you don't know, how did you find out about the paint?" I asked impatiently.

"Becky told me," said Patty, pointing at a little girl who had more purple on her than all the others put together.

I squatted down in front of Becky and asked for a description of Zippo. Batting her long curly eyelashes at me and leaning her head to one side, she lisped, "Zippo is a longleggity monster with google eyes, and he's bad-bad-bad, and he lives under the piano."

I looked under the piano. Sure enough, along with a lot of dust and a few broken crayons, there was a big puddle of purple paint.

Patty was a nervous wreck from then on. Personally, I think she excited the Tinies, whereas Lafayette, when she was around, had a calming influence. At any rate, I had them all buttoned up and out on the steps by three o'clock. None of this hanging around chatting with parents for me!

Patty breathed a sigh of relief when the last Tiny had left, clutching his mother's hand with tiny purple fingers. "I need a drink!" she announced.

I agreed. "An ice cream soda ought to do the trick."

Patty said ice cream wasn't exactly what she had in mind, but it would do just as well. We both had jumbo sodas, which was why we got home a little later than usual that afternoon. In fact, it was four-thirty by the time we walked up the front steps and Patty, still licking her lips, noticed a white envelope sticking out from under the doormat.

She ripped it open while I was unlocking the front door, and one glance at the page inside wiped the contented look from her face. "Oh, no!" she gasped. "The dirty rats— If that isn't just the limit!"

I snatched the letter away and read it quickly. It was from

the board of trustees of Saint Michael's Church, and it was short and sweet. Due to some long-overdue repairs planned for the basement of the church, which would involve moving all furniture, etc., out of the premises, the trustees regretted having to inform Mrs. Patty McFee that the Tiny Fingers Preschool Playgroup must move to a new location as of October 20.

"October twentieth?" Patty shrieked. "But that's next Monday!"

"Oh, pooh!" I said. "They can't do that to you. It isn't legal. Aren't you protected by your lease or something?"

"L-Lease?" Patty stammered. Her face was blank. "I didn't— I mean, nobody told me—that is, it was just a makeshift arrangement."

I stamped my foot. "Makeshift? You've been there for I don't know how many years and you call it makeshift? Your trouble is, you're so softhearted that everybody takes advantage of you!"

Patty sank down on the doorstep and held her head in her hands. "Oh, Zannah!" she wailed. "What are we going to do now?"

"You should have thought of this ages ago," I said. "It kills me to think that most of those Tinies have parents who earn millions sitting around doing nothing, while you and Lafayette work like slaves to take care of their kids, and they complain if you ask for an extra fifty cents, and now they're even kicking you out of the church."

"The trustees are kicking me out," Patty reminded me. "Not the parents."

"I bet those trustees are rich, too," I said. "Listen, I have a great idea. Marry a rich trustee and you'll never have to work again."

I wasn't really serious about the rich trustee because I had something better up my sleeve. We were going to pack up and move to the Hunky-Dory Dairy, where Patty would marry Hector Graybeal and teach the Noahs how to read.

Utopia Graybeal wasn't going to have a room of her own after all because, like it or not, she would be sharing it with me—her sister.

CHAPTER 4

I HOPED to have things settled by the twentieth, but it wasn't actually that easy. In the first place, Patty refused to take me out of school, even when I told her that teaching me herself with only five other children would be the best possible thing for my education.

"I couldn't teach the six of you at once anyway," she said. "You're all at different stages."

"That's the whole point," I argued. "In our school they call it mixed levels and they do it on purpose. Here's your chance for small-group activities."

"Here's my chance for chaos," said Patty.

In the second place, she refused to sell the house and move out to the dairy, on the grounds that the dairy didn't really exist, and she'd feel silly telling all her friends that we were moving to the nineteenth century. I didn't bother to argue that one with her, because I was sure I could win her over after I worked out the practical problems.

My big obstacle was that Patty wouldn't give up the Tiny Fingers Preschool Playgroup. Instead of sending letters around saying that due to the stinky, underhanded board of trustees the school would have to shut down, she called up all the parents and told them she would be teaching temporarily in her own home. Temporarily! I knew what that meant. It meant wet mittens on our radiator and finger paint on our walls, and it might go on for years.

"Patty, you can't *do* this to yourself!" I said. "Life is too short."

But I simply couldn't make her change her mind. In the end I decided the only solution was to bring her to the dairy as often as I could, arrange things so she would see as much as possible of Hector Graybeal, and let nature take its course.

It was hard to concentrate on school that week. I'm a good student, so my work didn't suffer, but my mind was on the Hunky-Dory Dairy.

All week long we found our milk, butter, and eggs on the front step in the morning. Patty remembered to put out the bottles and always left a slip of paper saying what we needed. I noticed that our consumption of dairy products almost doubled, but that was fine with me. Patty had taken to baking cakes and cooking exotic soufflés and quiches, instead of buying frozen food. It was obviously good for her health because her cheeks began to glow and she was in a good mood in spite of things going from bad to worse at the Tiny Fingers Preschool Play-group. I used to have to shake her awake again ten minutes after her alarm had gone off, but now she bounced out of bed and was downstairs making breakfast before I was dressed myself. Sometimes she was even out on the steps waiting when Mr. Pratt stopped by to deliver the milk.

On Saturday morning the van was late. We were out of cream, so Patty had to take her coffee black. She was already on her third cup when we finally heard a rattle of bottles. Patty fluffed her curls up a bit and hurried to the door.

"It's about time!" she told Mr. Pratt. "Come in and have some breakfast. What's new at the dairy?"

Pratt acted as if he hadn't eaten breakfast for a year. He took seconds of eggs and sausages, and after he had cleaned his plate Patty whipped up some pancake batter and made him start all over. Patty isn't the earth-mother type; it's not like her to force food on people, let alone do her own cooking. But I could see it was the best way she could find to keep him talking. The more stories he told about life at the Hunky-Dory Dairy, the more her eyes sparkled.

"Today is Saturday," I said. "Couldn't we go and visit? I bet Utopia has finished *The Secret Garden*. Do you think she'd like the Narnia books?"

Mr. Pratt said she probably would, if we could smuggle them past Hector Graybeal, but he had one more errand to run before returning to the dairy. "Unless you happen to have four yards of stuff around the house," he added, studying his list.

"We have *miles* of stuff," I said. "What kind do you need?"

"It's for Utopia," he said. "She wants it dark and serviceable."

It turned out that Utopia meant cloth. She needed a new winter dress, and Mrs. Noah had offered to make one for her.

Patty laughed. "Can Marigold sew? Somehow she doesn't seem the type."

"She never has, but she's willing to give it a try," said Mr. Pratt.

"Oh, no!" I said. "Poor Utopia! Wait, I have an idea."

I ran up to my room and came back with the Narnia books and one of my own dresses. I would have liked to give her my plaid jumper, but I chose a plain, navy blue dress with long sleeves that wouldn't shock her father.

"You don't care, do you, Patty?" I asked when I saw my mother's troubled face. "I've got plenty of dresses, and even if Utopia had the money to buy one ready-made, she'd have nowhere to buy it."

Patty shook her head doubtfully. "It's not that I care. It's just I wonder what's going on in their minds. They've apparently accepted the fact that they can't get out, but how do they think we get in, and where do they think we come from? If I were Marigold, I'd be asking a million questions, but she's the soul of discretion."

"They're all scared silly of that man Rudge," said Mr. Pratt. "First time I turned up, all they wanted to know was whether he had sent me. When I said I'd never heard of the guy, they dropped the subject. It took me months to get their own story out of them. They're a tight-lipped bunch—it's as if they were afraid Rudge could hear every word they say."

Patty let down the hem of my blue dress to make it look more old-fashioned, and I modeled it for Mr. Pratt.

"Won't get by," he said after careful scrutiny. "Too much flesh showing."

Peering down at my legs I had another idea. "How about jeans?" I suggested. "They're the same color. If Utopia wore jeans underneath, her father might think they were pantaloons."

I wore a kilt over my jeans that day, and Patty put on a frontier skirt that was longer than most of the things she wears. We weren't dressed like our usual Saturday selves, but we thought we'd blend in better at the dairy. We must have looked old-fashioned, or at least eccentric, because people kept turning and smiling as we drove through the streets of Burleith, all three of us perched in a row behind the dapple-gray mare.

Unfortunately, Patty spoiled the picture. It was a hot day for October, and as we went through Hector Graybeal's kitchen door she peeled off her sweater and knotted it casually around her waist. Underneath she was wearing an old pink T-shirt that said, "A Woman Needs a Man Like a Fish Needs a Bicycle."

I gasped but it was too late to warn her. Hector Graybeal

rose halfway from his armchair, turned purple in the face, and sank down with a growl.

Patty suddenly caught on and laughed. "Gracious!" she said. "Marigold had better lend me an apron. It's too hot for a sweater. How are you, Hector? And what on earth are you doing crowded into this kitchen on such a beautiful morning?"

They were all there. Hector Graybeal had been reading from a heavy, leather-bound Bible to the five children who were lined up solemnly on two long wooden benches: Japheth, Ham, and Loyal in front, Shem and Utopia behind. Mrs. Noah was at the stove, stirring a bubbling pot of something that smelled as if it had been overcooked for quite a while. Her hair was more of a mess than usual, and she wore her apron back to front.

Patty found a second apron on a hook by the door and slipped it over her head. The bib part covered the writing on her T-shirt, and I thought she looked quite proper again, but Hector Graybeal stood up, shook his head, and slammed the Bible shut.

"But Hector," Mrs. Noah squeaked. "Aren't you going to continue the lesson? You've only just begun."

"Woman, thy name is procacity!" he bellowed, and he slammed the door.

Mrs. Noah sighed. "Oh, dear! I do wish he would call me 'Marigold.' "

"What's procacity?" I asked.

Mrs. Noah looked at me vaguely and poked at a straggling curl with the handle of a wooden spoon.

"Oh, never mind," I said. "But why is he such a stamping and slamming person? I wouldn't put up with it for a minute!"

Mrs. Noah's mouth dropped open, but Patty giggled. "He needs a bossy daughter like you to keep him in line, Zannah."

I couldn't have agreed more, but I wasn't about to discuss it in front of the whole crowd. Instead I suggested that Patty take over Hector Graybeal's class.

"They're all there waiting," I said. "How about a reading lesson?"

"Not just now," said Patty. "I think Marigold needs me more than they do. What on earth are you making, Marigold?"

"Stew," said Mrs. Noah. She bent over the pot and sniffed doubtfully as a puff of black smoke rose from the bubbles.

"Stew can be tricky," said Patty. "Let's throw it out and start over."

I offered to take the children through their times tables, but at the mere mention of math they rose in a body and rushed out. I decided that this was as good a time as any to let Utopia in on my plans for Patty and her father.

"This is a deathly secret," I panted, running after Utopia into the barnyard. "Where can we be alone?"

Utopia led me through the barn and up a rickety ladder to the hayloft. I expected we would sit on the hay and talk, but she put her finger to her lips and motioned me over to the wall where, heaving the hay aside, she uncovered a passage into a room barely large enough for the two of us to sit down.

There was no window, but the wooden boards at the side of the barn had dried and weathered, letting sunlight filter in with slanted, dusty shafts. I squinted through the cracks and saw the meadow, and the pond where Loyal had tried to outwit a duck. Loyal was there again, with the two younger Noahs. Their trousers were rolled up to the knees and they were leaping in the mud.

"Is this your secret place?" I asked. "What a fantastic hideout! Who else knows about it?"

Utopia sighed. "Nobody, now. I had two friends before we were removed. They were girls my age, like you. We used to meet here, but now we can't, of course. I don't suppose they have the slightest idea where we were removed to."

Although I understood what she meant now, I laughed thinking how crazy it was to be talking that way. In my own life people moved, or families, but in Utopia's life a whole farm had moved: meadow, houses, and all, and it didn't seem to surprise her one bit.

I was dying to ask how it had felt to be magicked away like that, but for the moment I had more urgent matters to discuss. After she had hidden the complete *Chronicles of Narnia* under an old crate in a corner and changed into her new dress and pantaloon-jeans, I broached the subject of our parents.

"Do you miss your mother, Utopia?" I asked.

She picked at a scab on her ankle and frowned. "Not truly," she said. "That is, not my true mother. I don't remember her well enough. But I miss the mother I imagine."

I could tell it was going to be a good talk. Leaning back against the wall, I gazed dreamily up at the rafters. "How do you imagine her?"

"Funny," Utopia said unexpectedly. "Teasing. Someone who makes jokes. No one laughs here, have you noticed?"

I nodded. "I suppose that's because you haven't seen outsiders for a long time, except for Mr. Pratt, and he doesn't count. Your father has gotten too big for his britches, and the rest of you are all afraid of him."

Utopia looked shocked. "Aren't all men like that? Mr. Rudge was, I remember. We were all terrified of him, even his wife. Father is mild as a baby, compared to Mr. Rudge. That's why I'm secretly glad we were removed. If only I could be sure he wouldn't come to visit!"

"Why should he do that?" I asked.

Utopia sighed. "He said he might, that's why. Before he

removed us, he told Father not to try and come back. Father said he had no mind to return because he'd have no more dealings with the devil. And Mr. Rudge looked angry fit to kill, and he said, 'I may drop in someday, Hector, just to make certain you stay put, and mark my words—my visit won't be a pleasant one!' "

I put my arm around her shoulders. "Utopia, did he tell you where you were going? Or—or when?"

She shook her head. "Only that we weren't to be a nuisance anymore, and how *could* we be? We can't get out. No one but Mr. Pratt and your mother and yourself has ever come in. So what does it matter where we are?"

"Or when," I said musingly.

Utopia laughed. "When? That's easy: we're now. When else should we be? And as for the rest, I'm afraid there isn't much we can do about it."

"Yes, there is," I said. "There's something we could both do about it, you and I. As long as we're smart, that is, and careful. And if it works out, we'll have the most glorious life, Utopia! Believe me, we'll both be happy forever and ever."

She stared at me, half terrified, but as I unfolded my plan her face relaxed, and when I stopped talking she threw her arms around me and squeezed. "Oh, Zannah!" she cried. "Do you really think it will work? I've been so lonely. Oh, Zannah!"

"Sure, it will work," I said confidently. "Just do what I say, and don't let them think *we're* doing it. Let them think they fell in love at first sight."

I had a thousand ideas in my head: clothes we could exchange, things we could do together, ways we would decorate our room. But just as I was about to get into all that, there was a bump and a rattle on the other side of the wall, followed by a slithering sound.

I grabbed Utopia and squeaked, but she just laughed. "Cats in the hayloft," she reassured me. "Come on, Zannah. There's so much I want to show you!"

The rest of that Saturday was the happiest time I'd had in my whole life. I forgot about Hector Graybeal, and Patty, and trying to improve our life-style. I took off my kilt and socks and joggers, and Utopia took off her new dress so that all she wore over the jeans was a camisole. We jumped in the hay and petted the new calf, and flirted with a litter of kittens that Utopia discovered in a warm corner of the dairy.

We ran outside, taking care not to let the others see us, and explored the meadow and the woods. Utopia climbed a maple tree and swore she would never wear skirts again, except in the presence of her father. She taught me a hymn, and I taught her to sing "Ninety-nine Bottles of Beer on the Wall." We walked all the way down to the canal, singing every song we knew. By the time we had changed back into our respectable selves and returned to the kitchen, the sun was sinking behind the trees.

Mrs. Noah met us at the kitchen door. Her hair had been tidied again, probably by Patty, and her cheeks were flushed. The kitchen smelled divine.

"Where have you been, Utopia?" she asked. She was trying to frown, but I could tell her heart wasn't in it. "Why, just look at you! There's straw in your hair, and you've cut your foot—has your father seen you?"

Utopia plucked at her hair, which she wore in a long braid. "I'm sorry. I forgot the time. I forgot everything! Am I very late?"

Patty came up behind Mrs. Noah and put her arm around her waist. "Late for lunch, but just in time for supper. Don't scold her, Marigold. Zannah hasn't had a day in the country like this since I can remember, and it's so good for them—where's the harm in it?"

Mrs. Noah shook her head, but she began to smile. "What's the world coming to?" she asked. "Run along to the barn, Utopia. The boys are out there milking. And when you're through, make sure you wash at the pump, every one of you. We're having guests for supper."

"You mean we can stay?" I asked. "Great! What are we having?"

Patty winked at me. "Something went a little wrong with the stew, so we changed the menu. Mushroom omelette with hollandaise sauce. Creamed spinach. Followed by crepes with apple butter."

"But your mother has been working too hard," said Mrs. Noah. "I'm so ashamed! Won't you persuade her to sit in the parlor now, and rest?"

Patty brushed some flour off her apron. "And leave you to do all the work by yourself? No way! I'm just shocked that Hector never gives you a hand in the kitchen."

Marigold looked scandalized at the idea, but then she grinned. "A woman needs a man," she said shyly, "like a fish needs a bicycle."

There were ten of us at supper with me and Mr. Pratt, and it was a rowdy meal. Hector Graybeal and Mrs. Noah sat at opposite ends of the long table in wooden armchairs, but the rest of us were elbow to elbow on benches. I sat across from Utopia between the younger Noahs, who kept leaning forward to shout at each other across my plate.

Ham and Japheth were as like as twins, but Ham was quick to inform me that he was a whole year older than Japheth. They

Utopia climbed a maple tree and swore she would never wear skirts again, except in the presence of her father.

were weasely-faced little kids with greenish eyes that glinted out of their pale, freckled skin. In fact they were smaller versions of their brother, except that they were forever squabbling and into mischief, whereas Shem was quiet and a little sulky.

Shem sat at the foot of the table next to his mother, but he spent the entire meal staring gloomily at Patty, who was at the other end, next to Hector Graybeal. He smiled just once that I could see, and that was when Mr. Graybeal took his first bite of omelette and growled, "Fancy fare!"

Patty only laughed at this and spooned another dollop of hollandaise sauce onto Mr. Graybeal's omelette. "It's nothing but eggs from your chickens and mushrooms from your woods," she said, "but if you think food has to taste bad to be godly, I'm sure we could salvage some of Marigold's stew."

I was afraid Mrs. Noah's feelings would be hurt, but I needn't have worried. She cupped her hand over her mouth, looked guiltily at Hector Graybeal, and giggled.

As for Mr. Graybeal, he scowled at Patty and then smiled in spite of himself. "Impudence!" he muttered, serving himself another helping of omelette.

At this, Shem dropped his fork with a clatter and pushed back his chair. He had hardly touched his food, although he gulped down glass after glass of apple cider.

Mrs. Noah looked up at him anxiously. "Aren't you hungry, Shem? But this is delicious! And there's dessert tonight, too—stay and try it."

"Fence needs mending," said Shem. "Forgot." And he shuffled out of the room.

Utopia was furious. "He's so rude! Why do you allow him to behave like that, Father? Mrs. McFee won't want to come back again."

"Never mind," said Patty. "He's just going through an awkward phase. All boys do, at that age."

I was about to point out that our neighborhood was full of thirteen-year-old boys who were polite and fun to be with, and not a single bit awkward. But it didn't seem kind to Mrs. Noah, so I changed the subject and started a game with Utopia and the three little boys.

"I packed my grandmother's trunk and in it I put an apple," I began.

Once the others understood the rules, they joined in. As we went through the alphabet I was surprised to see that although Loyal and Utopia couldn't remember half the things we packed in our grandmother's trunk, Ham and Japheth rattled through the list without a moment's hesitation. Loyal and Utopia had dropped out by the time we got to *H*, but they cheered me on while I struggled with my turn.

"I packed my grandmother's trunk and in it I put an apple, a button, a calf, a dairy, an elm tree, a feather, my grandmother, and—um—a helicopter!" I shouted.

The grown-ups were talking too loud to overhear, but the children gaped at me in astonishment.

"A hell what?" Loyal whispered finally, after a worried glance at his father.

"Not hell—helicopter!" I said, beginning to laugh.

"What's that?" demanded Ham and Japheth.

"Oh, for goodness sake, haven't you ever seen a helicopter?" I asked. "It flies like an airplane, except—"

Then I saw Utopia's face. It was grave and wide-eyed, and she shook her head at me ever so slightly.

"It's just a long word," I told the boys. "A nothing word for fun, like procacity, whatever that is."

The boys were satisfied and we finished the game, after I had changed helicopter to handkerchief, but I worried about that expression on Utopia's face. How much had she guessed?

I soon found out. After supper she and I stayed alone in the kitchen while she washed the dishes and I dried.

"I hope you didn't mind my talking nonsense with the boys," I told her. "Sometimes I get silly."

Utopia looked up from the pan of soapy water and smiled. "You needn't tell me stories, Zannah. I won't give you away. I know you're from another planet, but you're very like us all the same, and what does it signify if we're friends?"

"Me?" I gasped. "From another planet?"

Utopia nodded. "You and your mother and perhaps Mr. Pratt, too, come to think of it. It never occurred to me, but that would explain his way of coming and going so easily when ordinary mortals can't get through at all."

"Ordinary mortals?" I repeated. I was completely dazed.

"Of course!" said Utopia. "So it's very fortunate that you found your way to our world, because I wanted a friend so badly. But we must take care that Father never finds out. He thinks it's witchcraft, you see. And if he had the courage to stand up to Mr. Rudge, just think what he would do to *you*!"

"But Utopia," I protested, "you have it backwards. *You're* from another world, not me. I belong here. In Washington, I mean, and the twentieth century. *You're* the ones who got removed to the wrong place and the wrong time."

Utopia refused to take me seriously. "Silly! We're ordinary, no different from everyone else. There were lots and lots of families on Mr. Rudge's farm, and they were all like us. But you and your mother, with your funny short hair and trousers, and time without clocks, and hell machines that fly through the air— well, I don't mind. I think it's exciting. But you'd better not let Father know, or he'll say you can't any of you come back."

I was silent for a while, trying to think how to explain. Meanwhile Utopia handed me the dishes one by one and kept on chattering.

"Please don't worry, Zannah! Why should it bother you if it doesn't bother me a bit? That pitcher goes on the shelf there, next to the sugar bowl. What's it like on your planet? If the girls look like boys, do the boys look like girls, or are you all alike?"

"We're all alike," I snapped. "Millions and millions of identical twins, and the gravity is upside down so we all stand on our heads, and we wear boot-gloves on our hands and sunbonnets on our feet."

Utopia roared with laughter. "Stop teasing! I don't believe you walk at all. You fly through the air in hell machines driven by devils. But I'm sure they're quite friendly little devils."

It occurred to me that I had never torn the copyright page out of the Narnia books. Perhaps if Utopia saw the dates she would believe we were in the twentieth century. "Come out to the barn," I said. "You know those books I brought you? There's something printed in them that proves I'm right."

Utopia said she couldn't leave the kitchen until she finished the baking pans, but I was impatient, so I set off to get the books myself.

It was already growing dark outside, and someone had hung a lantern in the dairy window. It cast a glow of orange light on the yard, where Patty was walking with Mrs. Noah and the two men. When she saw me she left them and ran over. Her arms were full of russet chrysanthemums that grew around the farmhouse, and she looked about ten years younger than she had that morning.

"Zannah, darling!" she cried. "Isn't this divine? Look at the flowers Marigold gave me to take home! But I swear, I could almost take your advice and stay here forever."

"Let's," I agreed. "They're all so nice! Especially Mr. Graybeal, don't you think? Isn't he the handsomest man you ever met?"

Patty looked surprised and burst out laughing. "He's a real

winner! But seriously, Zannah, we have to start home soon. There are no lights on the van, and Mr. Pratt wants to be out of the woods before it gets much later."

"I'll be ready in a minute," I promised. "I just have to get something for Utopia."

It was dark in the barn. I had to grope my way past the box stalls until I bumped up against the ladder. The cows shifted their weight heavily and I could hear wings flapping high up under the eaves—owls, or bats. It was so spooky that I sang Utopia's hymn to keep my courage up.

Still singing, I pulled myself up the ladder rung by rung until suddenly, halfway to the loft, a hand grabbed my ankle.

For a moment I thought I was going to fall. "Who's that?" I shrieked.

A low voice answered jeeringly. "Singing!"

I practically fainted from relief; it was only Shem. "Yes, singing," I said. "What's it to you?"

I didn't want Shem to find Utopia's hideout. Climbing back down and peering at him crossly, I tried to make out his face in the dark. "What do you think you're doing, coming up behind me like that? I could have broken my neck, you creep!"

Shem made a noise in his throat that might have been a particularly nasty laugh. "Singing," he repeated. "Don't sing, Zannah. Nothing to sing about. You don't belong here, or your mother either."

His voice gave me the shivers, but I was determined not to let him see how he had frightened me. "You people don't belong here either, if it comes to that."

Shem took me by the shoulders and gave me a shake. "Watch out, Zannah! We don't need you here, making trouble. Stay away or I'll make you sorry—you and your mother both!"

I could hear Patty calling me from outside in the yard. Shoving Shem away, I stumbled toward the door of the barn.

CHAPTER 5

IT RAINED again on Monday. Before leaving for school, I gave Patty some sound advice on keeping the Tinies' rain gear within six inches of the front door and confining the kids to one or maybe two rooms at the most.

"Whatever you do, don't let them in my room," I warned her. "I'd keep them out of the upstairs bathroom, too, if I were you. And if you care about your slipcovers, no finger painting in the living room. Come to think of it, why not make them come in the back door and stay in the kitchen all day? Then we can just hose it down when they go home."

"The kitchen is hardly big enough for you and me, let alone ten kids," said Patty. "Besides, Lafayette would be too close to the refrigerator and she's putting on a pound a day as it is."

"There may be ten kids the first day, but I bet you're down to two by the end of the week," I told her. "What parents would be crazy enough to send their kids to a setup like this? It's probably illegal and I *know* it's unhygienic."

Patty started laughing. "It wouldn't be quite so unhygienic if you put your breakfast dishes in the sink. Now, stop fussing over me, Zannah. I have a feeling this is going to be a success."

She was right. Three more kids joined the group on Thursday, and another had been signed up to start a week later. The new Tiny Fingers Preschool Playgroup was not only a success, but it was also getting rave reviews in our neighborhood. Some dreamer had the idea of describing it as "an adventure in home communications," whatever that means, and parents began calling up to ask if there was a long waiting list.

So far I hadn't had a chance to observe the playgroup in its new location because I left for school before the Tinies arrived and came back after they had gone. Of course they left a few traces, like Play-Doh in the toaster and peanut butter on the African violet, but I never came home on time to see the Tinies in action.

On the last Friday in October, however, I woke up with a cold and Patty ordered me to stay in bed. It's annoying, how she only lets me stay in bed when I'm not feeling good enough to enjoy it. I lay there for a while feeling sorry for myself, but soon I was distracted by a strange noise from below. It sounded like a giant gerbil nibbling on a giant toilet paper tube. Stuffing my bathrobe pockets with Kleenex, I set off to investigate and found the source of the noise halfway down the stairs. It was Becky, sawing at one of the banister bars with a steak knife. She had already made a fairly good dent in the wood, and there were flecks of paint and sawdust all over the carpet on the stairs.

"Hey, quit that, you dummy!" I said, prying the knife out of her hands. Before I could finish telling her off, I had a fit of coughing.

Becky was outraged. "Cover your mouth!" she ordered. "I hate germs, and I *need* that knife."

"What for?" I asked, holding the knife behind my back.

"Zippo needs to get out of here," said Becky. "He hates this place, so I'm helping him escape."

"There's an easier way out," I told her. "Come on, I'll show you."

I led Becky downstairs and through the living room, where

we had to edge our way around Patty and three other Tinies who were standing on their heads, trying to recite the alphabet backwards.

"Here we go!" I said, opening and shutting the front door. "Bye-bye, Zippo! Don't call us, we'll call you."

Becky watched me scornfully. "That wasn't Zippo, that was Bingo," she said. "Bingo likes it here." She opened the door again and let Bingo back in.

Behind me Patty chanted, "—E-D-C-B-A!" and stood right side up again. She was very red in the face. "How are you feeling, Zannah?"

"Great!" I said. "Just fantastic! Who needs to breathe?"

"Go back to bed," said Patty.

"I don't feel safe in bed," I complained. "Not with Mack the Knife here wandering around. Where's Lafayette?"

"She called to say she didn't feel up to it this morning," said Patty. "No problem, I'm doing just fine. What's Becky been up to?"

"Small-group activities," I said, handing her the knife. "Does your insurance cover Zippo and Bingo?"

Patty said that come to think of it she wasn't sure *any* of them were insured, now that the playgroup had moved to our house. She went to the telephone to find out about it, leaving me in charge of the Tinies. I was afraid they would scatter and get into thirteen different kinds of mischief so I told them to form a circle and all hold hands, but I should have known it wasn't that simple to organize kids. Becky refused to cooperate unless she was between Zippo and Bingo, and the Tinies on the other sides of Zippo and Bingo said it was creepy to hold a hand they couldn't see.

Becky's feelings were so hurt that she left the circle. "Anyway," she said, "Zippo and Bingo need to pee. How do you get to the upstairs bathroom?"

I barred the way. "You don't need the upstairs bathroom. There's one down here."

"That's the girls' room," said Becky. "Zippo is a boy."

"Tough!" I said. "If you don't want him in with you and Bingo, he'll just have to wait his turn."

Becky decided she and Bingo would wait and let Zippo go first. I was dumb enough to think I had settled the problem, so I went to the kitchen to get some juice. Meanwhile Becky and Bingo grew tired of waiting for Zippo to come out of the downstairs bathroom so they went to the upstairs one after all, and Becky wrote "Bingo loves Zippo" all over the mirror with Patty's lipstick. At least that's what she told me it said. It looked like scribbling to me.

"Don't you screen the kids who come to your school?" I asked Patty after I had cleaned up the mess. "Can't you give them blood tests or something to find out whether they're weird or hyper?"

"Once a child is happy with us, he adjusts," Patty murmured. She was stuffing baby-food jars with wet cotton for a seed-sprouting project.

"Bingo likes it here, but Zippo hates it," I informed her.

"Be patient," Patty said vaguely. "Give him time to adjust. Then he'll feel happier."

Looking at the clock, I realized that it was getting close to noon. The idea of sharing peanut butter and milk with fifteen Tinies, two of whom were invisible, made me wish I had gone to school that day after all. I felt a little guilty walking out on Patty, but I got dressed, built myself a club sandwich, and slipped out the back door.

It was a beautiful day. If my nose hadn't been stuffed up I would have really enjoyed playing hooky, but it's hard to ignore a stuffed-up nose. To make things worse, the Kleenexes were in my bathrobe pockets, so I had the choice of looking at the sky all the time or using my sleeve. I alternated. When the sidewalk was clear I gazed upwards and tried to feel exalted about the autumn foliage, but when the going got rough or I had to cross a street, I looked down and used my sleeve.

I didn't pay much attention to where I was going, except for avoiding places where people might recognize me and ask why I wasn't in school. It came as a surprise when I reached the corner of 42nd Street and ahead of me, leading into Archbold Glover Park, was the dirt track to the Hunky-Dory Dairy.

I hesitated. It had never occurred to me to try and get to the dairy on my own. In fact I had assumed that it wasn't possible, because the time Patty drove me around in the car we couldn't find the track at all. But it was there today, and I was dying to have a chat with Utopia about Shem. Why had he threatened me that night in the barn? Why didn't he want me to come to the dairy? Everyone else was friendly. Why wasn't Shem?

The problem was, Patty had forbidden me to go into the woods alone. Even if she were crazy enough to allow it, I wouldn't have wanted to go. Lonely woods in the middle of the city just aren't safe.

But if the track to the dairy was there, then the woods weren't in the city anymore. They were in the country, back in the nineteenth century. Or were they?

I took a few steps in and turned to see if anyone had noticed me. Cars were going back and forth on 42nd Street and people strolled by on the sidewalk, but no one paid the slightest attention to me or the fact that a dirt track had suddenly appeared where there wasn't one before. I had a suspicion that the track and I were both invisible, now that I was in dairy territory.

Very cautiously, trying to stay under cover and make as little noise as possible, I continued into the woods. The air was still.

City sounds gave way to the sound of birds singing and a stream trickling somewhere not too far off. My feet thumped on the path and my heart thumped in my chest. I was tempted to run hard and get the scary part over with, but I knew that if I ran I might not hear if there was any danger.

Suddenly there were footsteps in the underbrush. I froze, and then backed quietly into the shelter of a bush. The steps came so close that I was sure I had been seen, but just when I was about to scream and make a mad dash for home, they stopped and someone started whistling.

Peering out through the leaves, I saw Shem a few yards away from me, at the foot of a maple tree. He gave a hitch to his trousers, spat on his hands, and shinnied up so fast that I guessed it wasn't the first time he had climbed that tree.

While he was climbing I burrowed even further into my bush and sat down. I wasn't taking any chances on Shem chasing me through those woods. No matter how long I had to sit there, I preferred to wait until he went away.

I don't know how long I sat and waited, but I certainly wasn't bored. Watching Shem was as good as the movies. After hoisting himself to a place where the branches forked, he stopped, looked around furtively, reached into a hole in the trunk, and drew out a small bundle.

I wasn't close enough to see what was inside, but I soon guessed. The smell of pipe smoke drifted down and tickled my nose until it was all I could do to keep from sneezing. Shem probably wouldn't have heard me if I did though, because he was talking too loud.

What had started as a mumble grew almost to a shout after Shem got his nerve up. What he was saying I wouldn't care to repeat. It was a mixture of swearing and praying. But basically he was asking God to keep Mr. Rudge—his own father—away from the dairy. Asking, and then threatening, and then pleading again, and all the while puffing away on that pipe. It was funny in a way, but it was scary, too. I was glad when he finally went away.

After Shem left I felt safe. It now seemed clear to me that he was the only danger in those woods, and I had watched him out of sight. I changed my mind about going home and continued toward the dairy, moving a little faster now and not being so careful about noise. In fact I even sneezed a few times, which slowed me down because I had to find some soft leaves. Leaves aren't as good as Kleenex, but they're better than your sleeve.

Pretty soon I came around a corner and saw the meadow ahead, bright green in the open sunlight. I sped up and was almost out of the woods when a hand reached out to grab my shoulder and a rasping voice called, "Caught you!"

This time I was more angry than surprised: it was Shem again.

"What are you doing here?" he demanded. "I thought I told you to stay away!"

"Oh, for heaven's sake!" I shouted, pushing his hand away. "You stop bullying me, Shem Rudge, or I'll tell Mr. Graybeal you've been smoking his pipe in the woods."

Shem snorted. "It's not his pipe. I borrowed it from my father."

"Borrowed? Hah!" I said. "I can guess what kind of borrowing it was. What would he do if he saw you smoking it?"

For an instant, the expression on his face turned to sheer terror.

I took pity on him. "Don't worry, I bet he never turns up. But if that's Mr. Graybeal's tobacco you're smoking, you'd better mind your manners or I'll tell him why his supply keeps running low."

I moved around Shem and started walking toward the dairy again. "Listen," I said. "You don't have to like me. I don't have to like you either, if it comes to that. But I'm not doing you any harm, am I? I'm not doing *anyone* any harm, I'm just Utopia's friend. So what's the problem?"

Shem followed me all the way to the dairy. He didn't say a single word, but every time I turned around I saw his scowling face, a few steps behind. I kept my cool and pretended I couldn't care less, and before long it turned out to be true. I really didn't care. But I was more anxious than ever to have a chat with Utopia.

Utopia gave me a mug of strong, sweet tea and a large handkerchief. "That's what comes of not wearing enough clothes," she scolded me. "When I went out to milk this morning there was frost on the grass. Would you like me to lend you a shawl?"

I sat on Utopia's bed while she rummaged in the wooden chest and pulled out a heavy, lumpy gray thing that looked as if it had been knitted by a child.

"No, Mrs. Noah made it," said Utopia when I asked. "It took her months, and she cried a tear for every stitch. Japheth was just a baby then, and he kept pulling out the needles. I knitted the next one myself. It's much nicer, don't you agree?"

Utopia's shawl was no less lumpy than the one she was teaching me to cross over my front and tie behind my back. The only difference was that my shawl was fairly clean, while Utopia's had bits of twigs and straw woven into the stitches. My guess was that she had knitted it outdoors.

"I love it!" I said, and I must admit that a shawl is a comfortable way to stay warm in chilly weather, once you've got it on correctly. It keeps you warm without getting in the way of your arms, a little the way a down vest does.

I noticed that Utopia was wearing my jeans under my old blue dress, and I reminded myself to put on a skirt again the next time I came, just to stay on the good side of Hector Graybeal.

"Oh, Utopia, I've got so much to tell you!" I said. "Come sit down."

"I can't," she said. "I'm making applesauce. We have to put up jars and jars of it, to last the winter. I've cut my fingers to shreds with peeling. Just look!" She held her hands out to show me all the nicks and scratches.

"Poor you!" I said. "Doesn't anybody help you?"

Utopia shrugged. "The little boys are supposed to peel, but I know for a fact that they've all three of them gone to the woods to find horse chestnuts. I'll swat their bottoms when they get back. I sent Shem to look and he was away for ages, but he said there wasn't a sign of them. You didn't catch sight of them on your way here, did you?"

"No," I said, "but I saw Shem. Just wait until you hear—"

"Not now," said Utopia. "If Father comes in and sees I'm not working I'll never hear the end of it. You can tell me in the kitchen."

"I'll help peel," I offered, following her downstairs.

A huge pot of sliced apples was stewing on the wood stove. Steam rose above them as they bubbled, and I could guess what a sugary smell I would be smelling if I didn't have a cold. Several baskets of apples waited on the kitchen table. I knew I had my work cut out for me.

"Watch for worms!" said Utopia. "Look—you missed one in this apple. And don't forget to slice them after you peel them. If you're sure you don't mind helping, that is."

"Don't the natives of your planet make applesauce?" Utopia asked.

"It's not that I mind," I said. "It's just that I'm not experienced. I'm sure I'll get better with practice."

"Don't the natives of your planet make applesauce?" Utopia asked. "I suppose you have all sorts of magical fruits that I never dreamed of. Tell me about them!"

I laughed. "My planet is your planet, only in the future. Why won't you believe me? Patty and I don't make our own applesauce. The applesauce at the supermarket is perfectly good, and it saves time."

Utopia immediately requested a description of a supermarket, so I told her about the long aisles, and the frozen food department, the coupons and checkout counters. She kept interrupting to ask more questions, and I was sidetracked into explaining about diet sodas and taco chips before I remembered what had been on my mind.

"Listen, I don't have time to tell you all that stuff now," I said. "Next time I come I'll bring you a Coke and some tacos. I'll bring you something new *every* time I come, as long as you don't tell the others. But right now I'm worried about Shem."

Utopia stirred the applesauce, listening seriously as I described first what happened in the barn and then Shem's behavior in the woods that day. She was shocked to hear about the stolen tobacco, but the rest of the story left her undisturbed.

"Shem is a tease," she said. "He didn't mean you any harm."

I shook my head. "You wouldn't say that if you'd seen his face. He doesn't like me or Patty either, and he wants us both out of here. If it wasn't for knowing I can make trouble for him about smoking in the woods, he'd think up all kinds of things to tell your father so we wouldn't be allowed to come back anymore. He probably doesn't even have to make them up. What do you bet he's been spying on us? He'll tell your father—"

I never got around to what Shem might tell Hector Graybeal because something tickled my nose. I sneezed three times all over my heap of apple slices, just as Mrs. Noah walked in the kitchen door.

"Zannah McFee!" she exlaimed. "Use your handkerchief, child. Oh, what a waste!"

She swept the contaminated slices into her apron and dumped them in the bucket where Utopia had put the peelings for the chickens.

"Sorry, Brs. Doah!" I said, blowing my nose into Utopia's cotton handkerchief.

Mrs. Noah laughed. "Where did you get that dreadful cold? You should be in bed. Does your mother know you're here?"

When she heard the answer she bustled me out the door, and that was the end of my little chat with Utopia.

I tried to get in a few more words, but Utopia wouldn't leave the stove.

"Don't worry," she said. "I'm sure you're making a fuss about nothing. It's probably because you're feverish. Hurry back to bed and I'll tell Shem to stop making such a nuisance of himself."

Shem didn't give her a chance to tell him anything. He was hanging around in the barnyard when I came outside, and the moment he saw me he started to trail me again, staying his usual three paces behind as I walked across the meadow. At times I was sure I could feel his hot breath on the back of my neck. It was enough to make me scream, but if his aim was to give me the creeps I certainly wasn't going to let him know he was succeeding.

Halfway through the woods we were ambushed. Loyal, Ham, and Japheth leaped out of the bushes, throwing horse chestnuts and letting out bloodcurdling screams. By that time my nerves were a wreck, so I jumped about a foot in the air. Then I relaxed. I was glad of their company.

"Hi, brats!" I said. "Want to walk partway home with me? Just don't get too near, or I'll give you my cold."

"Where *is* your home, Zannah?" asked Loyal. "Why can you come and go when we can't? Are you sent by Mr. Rudge?"

I could have killed him. If Shem got *that* idea into his head, he'd hate me more than ever. "Of course not, silly!" I told him. "Patty and I are good, not evil. Good—like Mr. Pratt. No traffic with the devil, get it?"

I felt pretty dumb, putting it like that, but I didn't go into more detail with Shem around.

As it was, he stepped protectively between the small boys and me as if I were about to tuck them into my club sandwich and eat them.

"They've got work to do," he growled. "Get moving, you three! Back to the kitchen or Mr. Graybeal will take a stick to you."

Loyal was unimpressed. "Father never beats us. He just sermonizes."

"Get moving!" Shem repeated. He stepped menacingly toward the little boys, but they laughed and darted away. It was obvious that escorting me through the woods sounded like more fun than peeling apples.

"Oh, get moving yourself, Shem!" I said. "Quit following me around or I'll spit on you and you'll catch my cold."

The little boys hooted with laughter and I saw in a flash that I should have kept my mouth shut. Shem had been heading for home, but now he swung around and lunged at me. I backed up a few steps and giggled, but inside I was terrified.

"Go away!" I shouted. "You don't scare me. You couldn't scare anybody! You're just a nuisance, that's all. An overgrown, uneducated nuisance!"

Before I had time to catch my breath, I was alone in the

woods. Loyal Graybeal and the three Noah boys had vanished into thin air, and what was worse, so had the track I was walking on. I was all alone in the middle of Archbold Glover Park without the slightest idea how to get home.

CHAPTER 6

W HEN PATTY took my temperature it was 103°. My mind got a little fuddled, so I don't remember too clearly how I found my way home, which is probably just as well because I *do* remember that it was awful. I ran like crazy and stumbled over things and must have gone straight through a patch of poison ivy because I was covered with a rash the next day.

I knew I was lost, but the one time I met someone, a perfectly friendly looking woman jogging with a dog, I was in such a panic that I turned and ran in the opposite direction. I finally came out on a street blocks and blocks out of my way, on the far side of the park. Not having a bus token or even money for a phone call, I had to walk home. By the time I got there I was hot and cold at the same time, and so glad to see Patty that I hugged her for every word of scolding she could get out.

"Too bad," said Patty when she brought a cup of hot chocolate to my room the next morning. "It's perfect weather for spending the day at the dairy. I'm dying to see Marigold! I found some easy recipes for her, and I bought her an eggbeater. Can you believe the woman has never laid eyes on an eggbeater? They existed back then, but her husband thought they were frivolous.

I wish I could get her an electric mixer, but it wouldn't be much use without electricity."

I sighed. "It's weird to think of all the things that have been invented since their time that they never even dreamed of. I bet they wouldn't even approve of a lot of them, if they knew."

"They'd be horrified," Patty agreed. "But how much do you think they really *want* to know about the world around them?"

"Utopia is the only one who wants to know anything at all," I said. "Except maybe for the little boys, and it wouldn't be safe to tell them. The others are too scared that Mr. Rudge will come back and punish them for trying to find out. Mr. Pratt says that newspaper I gave you was the last they ever saw, and they never ask him to bring one. They don't even dare read the papers anymore!"

"They'd get a shock if they did," said Patty. "But that dreadful man would be dead by now. I wish there were some way we could prove it to them."

"Let's not try," I said pessimistically. "We'd only make things worse."

Patty laughed. "You really do feel down, don't you! How about wrapping in a blanket and sitting in the backyard for a while when the sun gets warmer? This would be a good day to plant some bulbs."

"Sure," I said, although the idea didn't appeal to me. "I'm sorry to spoil your fun, Patty. It wasn't much fun for me yesterday either, if that's any consolation."

Consolation came in another form. Mr. Pratt turned up at around eleven and invited us both for a picnic. Not to the dairy this time, but down by the Potomac River. He said we could rent bicycles, or maybe a canoe. Patty refused at first, but I convinced her that I'd be fine all by myself. I had homework to catch up on, and there was a good movie later that afternoon on television.

"I might even sleep," I said. "If you stayed home, you'd just make a lot of clatter and keep me awake. I mean it!"

Patty gave in and went downstairs to make some sandwiches. She brought me a tray before she left, and she looked as excited as a little kid.

"I'm so glad I saved that lobster salad!" she said. "We're going to have lobster rolls, and avocado slices, and fruit salad, and Camembert cheese with French bread. Pretty classy, hmmm? And Mr. Pratt has a bottle of white wine on ice. I put a sample of everything on your tray."

"Including the wine?" I asked.

"Excluding the wine," said Patty, "but I made you *squeezed* orange juice to celebrate."

"Celebrate what?" I asked. "Is this my last meal or something?"

"Oh, just the weather," said Patty. "It's such glorious weather! But never mind, next time you'll come along, too."

There was too much mayonnaise on the lobster rolls, and the avocado made me feel like throwing up. I could smell the Camembert even through my cold so I put it outside my door, but I managed to get down some French bread. Later that afternoon I tottered out of bed and hid the rest of my lunch at the bottom of the garbage so Patty's feelings wouldn't be hurt.

"Did you have a good time?" I asked when she came home.

"Gorgeous!" said Patty. "We didn't rent bikes after all. We just walked for miles and miles up the towpath and had lunch on the banks of the canal. We watched a man fishing, and it was so funny, Zannah! Peter asked if they were biting, and the guy answered—"

"Peter?" I repeated. "Peter who?"

"Peter Pratt, of course," said Patty. "I thought you knew his name was Peter."

"Well, I didn't," I said, "and I bet you didn't either before today. What did the fisherman say?"

"Oh, nothing," Patty said vaguely. "We had fun, that's all. How about you?"

She fluffed up my pillow, brushed the crumbs off my sheets, scooped up half a dozen empty juice glasses, and wandered away, humming.

By Monday my cold was getting better, but I still wasn't ready to go back to school. I felt well enough to come down and help out with the playgroup, though. It was a good thing, because for once Lafayette turned up. I hadn't seen her for ages, and as soon as I laid eyes on her, I knew that her problem wouldn't be solved by Weight Watchers.

"Hi, Lafayette!" I said when she walked through the front door. "When's your baby due?"

Lafayette grinned down at her bulging stomach and gave it a proud little tap. "December 25. Cross your fingers that it's right on time. Don't you think it'd be fabulous to have a kid on Christmas Day?"

"Fabulous for you," I said. "You save money on presents. For the kid, it's a disaster."

"Nothing's going to be a disaster for any kid of mine," said Lafayette, and I knew she was right. If she was as nice to her baby as she was to the Tinies, he was in luck. She'd probably give him double the usual amount of presents and throw in a birthday party as well.

Later I took Patty aside. "You're in trouble," I said. "She's seven months pregnant. There's no way she's going to work right up to Christmas. She isn't much use to you even now, you've got to admit."

"She sits down a lot," Patty agreed, "but you can hardly blame her."

"I wouldn't be surprised if she had quintuplets," I predicted gloomily. "Watch out! She'll bring them to work, and you're so softhearted you'll probably end up changing all their diapers. When are you going to learn to stick up for yourself?"

"Don't count your quintuplets before they hatch," said Patty. She began to enumerate Lafayette's good points: how patient she was with the Tinies, how she baked a cake every time one of them had a birthday, and that kind of stuff.

"Sure, I know," I said, interrupting her. "I never said I didn't like her, I just said she isn't going to be here. You can't run this place by yourself, can you? Parents are always checking up on the student–teacher ratio, aren't they? What are they going to say when they find out it's one to thirteen?"

"One to twenty-four," Patty corrected me, smiling.

"Help!" I said. "Are Zippo and Bingo bringing all their friends?"

Patty told me she was expanding the playgroup, starting the first of the new year. There were at least a dozen new families on the waiting list, and she had already started plans for turning the basement into a gigantic playroom with special kitchen and bathroom facilities, and the kind of floor that's easy to clean.

It was exasperating. What was the use of going to all that trouble? If my own plans went right it was only a matter of weeks before Hector Graybeal would convince Patty to give up the playgroup altogether and move to the Hunky-Dory Dairy.

"I'd think twice about that if I were you," I said. "There are probably zoning laws against that sort of thing."

"I've already been to see those people," said Patty. "Everything's all lined up. The contractor says the place is ideal for converting. He says he can do the whole job in ten days."

"Contractor!" I wailed. "Patty, you can't be serious—think of what it will cost! Who needs it? You won't have Lafayette to help you anymore. You probably won't find *anyone* to take on a job like that. You wear yourself out for thirteen of those brats already. What will your life be like when you're stuck with double that many?"

"Only twenty-four," Patty said gently, "and I've got the staff lined up, too."

"Who?" I demanded.

"I'll tell you all about it later," said Patty. "Don't worry, Zannah. You're a big help; you always will be. But I'm old enough to leave the nest."

That afternoon Mr. Pratt came by to drop off a jar of apple-sauce and a letter from Utopia. "Can't stay," he said hurriedly. "Have to go back and finish up some work at the office. But Utopia said she'd kill me if I didn't get this to you right away."

"That was really nice of her," I said. "I helped her make it, you know."

"Not the applesauce," said Mr. Pratt. "The letter. She said to read it and give me an answer, so I can bring it tomorrow morning early. I hope you're not up to mischief. Never knew Utopia to write a letter before."

"I suppose she never had anyone to write to," I said.

The letter was sealed with some messy kind of wax instead of being in an envelope. The outside had already been written on. Printed, in fact: it was an old business letter to Mr. Rudge about a horse-drawn reaper, but inside was a message scrawled with what I guessed from all the blots and scratches must have been the kind of pen you have to dip into a bottle of ink:

Dear Zannah.

A dreadful thing has occurred. Shem saw you disappear and claims it is witchcraft. Are you gone forever? If not how shall we explain? Write immediately with sincere regards.

Utopia Graybeal

I groaned.

"What is it?" Patty demanded anxiously. "Bad news, darling?"

"Nothing I can't take care of. But that Shem Rudge is making a real nuisance of himself. Would you believe he—"

I caught my breath. What had I just said? Shem had been making a nuisance of himself! But Mr. Pratt had told us that the Hunky-Dory Dairy had been magicked away a century ago to a time and place where they *couldn't* make a nuisance of themselves. And Patty had said the reason the three of us could see them when no one else could was that to us they weren't a nuisance at all. Until last Friday, that is. On Friday in the woods I had called Shem Rudge a nuisance, and all four boys had disappeared. I had vanished from their sight, too, according to Utopia's letter. Would I ever see them again?

"Hurry up, Zannah," said Mr. Pratt. "I have to get back to work. Not that I'm fond of my job, but for pride's sake I'd rather quit than be fired."

I tore a sheet of paper from my school notebook. "I'm still here," I wrote. "Tell Shem smoking gives you visions. I'll explain later. Love, Zannah."

I didn't want to worry Utopia, but I wasn't at all sure I'd ever have a chance to explain. What if the mare stopped at the edge of the woods next time Mr. Pratt tried to take me to the dairy, the way she stopped when he had tried to take the other children out? What if the dirt track wasn't there for me at all? As soon as Mr. Pratt left, I confided in Patty.

Patty listened very seriously with her brow wrinkled and her head held in her hands. "It sounds as if you're right," she said when I got through. "It's the only explanation I can think of, at any rate. But it may not be too late to do something about it. Would there be any way you could *un*think Shem as a nuisance?"

"I've been unthinking as hard as I can," I said. "Believe me, Shem can do and say whatever he likes from now on and I'll adore him for it, as long as I can keep on going to the dairy."

"It's the witchcraft that bothers me," said Patty. "We've got to get that idea out of their heads. I tell you what—let's invite them all for dinner."

"Are you crazy?" I said. "They can't any of them get out, and if they could and they saw what kind of world we live in, then they'd *really* think it's witchcraft."

"I know that, silly," said Patty. "What I mean is, we'll prepare a feast and take it to the dairy. As a kind of peace offering. And while we're there, I have a little plan that might just help straighten things out."

We were already into November. The days were going by fast, the way they usually do at that time of year, and Patty seemed to be making more progress with her plans than I was with mine. I was absolutely sure that if Utopia and I could bring our parents together, they'd be the happiest grown-ups in the world. I admit I had my own happiness in mind, too, but from Patty's point of view wouldn't that be even better? It was frustrating to think I had been able to make only four trips so far, and two of them without Patty. If only we could go more often! But Patty had her playgroup and I had school, so the only hope was weekends.

I had to work extra hard the rest of that week at school. There had been a test on Friday of the week before, and a paper had been assigned for Tuesday that I didn't even know about. I stayed up late every night trying to catch up, and things weren't made any easier by the fact that my friends decided I was giving them the cold shoulder. Actually I had only two or three friends—no one as close to me as Utopia or Patty, come to think of it. All the same, I didn't like the way those few were turning their backs on me and whispering at recess. As Mr. Pratt had said, for pride's sake I'd rather quit than be fired.

While I caught up on my homework, Patty was zooming ahead with her plans for converting our basement into a Tiny Fingers paradise. It was discouraging, but on the other hand she was equally excited about our feast at the Hunky-Dory Dairy, so I didn't know what to think.

On Monday night, Patty had tucked an envelope in among the empty milk bottles. It was an extremely formal letter to Mrs. Noah begging the favor of entertaining the Rudges and the Gray-beals at their own home for Saturday night dinner.

"Where do the Noahs live?" I asked. "It never occurred to me."

"In rooms over the dairy," said Patty. "Peter says they're more comfortable than the farmhouse, really, but I've never seen them."

"I wish you'd stop calling him 'Peter,' " I said. "It seems disrespectful. Is he coming to the party, by the way?"

"Of course he is," said Patty. "He's driving us. You weren't planning to walk there and back, were you?"

I was working on an overdue science report so I didn't have time to argue with Patty. I helped her in the kitchen whenever I could, though, and I've never seen such preparations in my life, not even for Thanksgiving or Christmas.

Patty used to be a shortcut cook. If something tasted good, she didn't care if it was frozen or packaged. She never let on to the guests, of course, but she wasn't above throwing in a can of soup and pretending the sauce was an old family recipe. This time, however, she made everything from scratch, so as not to be accused of witchcraft. There was watercress soup, followed by fish in aspic with homemade mayonnaise, followed by glazed pork with peach dressing, followed by a frosted angel cake and pudding with a French name to make it fancy.

Patty gave the dressing a final stir and wiped her hands on her jeans, leaving a disgusting streak of flour and butter. "This tastes better with fresh kiwis," she informed me, "but I don't trust kiwis. I suspect they might be classed as witchcraft. The peaches are canned, I have to confess, but they might conceivably have been canned by us."

I put my finger in the sauce and licked it. "It's fabulous!"

"Thanks. It's out of my French cookbook," said Patty. "Most of the meal is, if it comes to that."

"Aren't you afraid Mr. Graybeal will think French is wicked?" I asked.

Patty laughed. "Give poor Hector a break, Zannah! He may seem a little stiff on the surface, but underneath he's an old sweetie."

My heart rose. It looked as if my plans were finally beginning to work! "It's going to be a fabulous, fabulous party!" I said, hugging Patty. "Wear something really pretty to it, promise? Wear your lacy blouse."

"Don't worry, I won't put you to shame," said Patty, and she fluffed up her curls with a pudding-smeared hand.

The one place Patty really cheated was the bread. She bought French bread from a French bakery. As we trotted along toward the dairy behind the dapple-gray mare, all three of us decked out in our Sunday best, I smiled to myself, wondering what Patty would say if Mrs. Noah asked her for the recipe.

We were bringing so many covered dishes and baskets of food

with us that neither Patty nor Mr. Pratt noticed I had added a basket of my own. Inside were a bottle of Coke, a bag of barbecue-flavored taco chips, a box of pale blue stationery complete with envelopes, and a set of marker pens. It was undoubtedly a twentieth-century collection, but I figured that in all the fuss we could smuggle it off to Utopia's hideout in the barn.

Patty held the angel cake on her lap as tenderly as if it were a newborn baby. I thought she looked irresistible in her long frontier skirt and the white, lacy blouse that came all the way up under her chin. She even wore a little straw hat on her head with two chrysanthemums tucked under its wide black band. The effect, however, was spoiled by her socks. She had wisely decided to cover the few inches of flesh showing above her ankles, but if I had noticed on time I would have advised her not to choose pink and green striped kneesocks.

Patty looked at me and smiled. "Excited, Zannah?"

"Am I ever!" I said. "When Mr. Graybeal tastes this meal, it'll hit him how many years he's wasted being a bachelor."

Mr. Pratt looked at me suspiciously. Then he laughed. "Let's sing!"

So we trotted through the streets of Burleith singing "The Old Gray Mare She Ain't What She Used to Be." People stared, but I didn't mind. What I minded was collecting so many dogs. By the time we turned off 42nd Street into the dirt track to the dairy, there were more than a dozen trailing along behind us, yapping and whining and teasing the mare. It was a little embarrassing, so I was relieved when they left us at the edge of the woods.

"Good riddance!" I said, looking back to watch the sunlit patch of street grow smaller as we advanced through the dark archway of trees.

Then I gasped. "Hey, I'm here! I got in after all!"

Patty winked. "Why do you think we had you singing? So you wouldn't worry about a thing. Keep your mind clear of nuisance and you'll do just fine."

"You've got it all figured out, haven't you!" said Mr. Pratt, putting his arm around Patty's shoulder.

"This crazy setup?" said Patty. "I'd be wasting my time and energy if I even tried. Now, no hanky-panky, Peter, or you'll shock Hector, and we wouldn't want that, would we?"

It turned out I wasn't the only one with a secret basket. As soon as we had deposited our meal on the kitchen table, Patty whisked Mrs. Noah off to her room over the dairy. Ten minutes later Mrs. Noah returned, totally transformed. She was wearing a long green corduroy skirt and a blouse almost exactly like Patty's, and although her cheeks might just have been flushed with excitement, I suspected Patty had been at work with her blush-on. In any case, those clothes were no hand-me-downs. I had never seen them in Patty's closet, and I went through it all the time looking for things to borrow.

"She looks beautiful!" I whispered. "Where did you get the skirt and blouse? Did you buy them?"

Patty nodded. "Ssssh! Let's see what Hector says."

"Meanie!" I said. "He'll kill her! She looks too pretty to be good."

But Hector Graybeal didn't kill Mrs. Noah. He didn't even notice her until we had all gathered around the table and she was standing directly opposite him. Then he stared. I held my breath, waiting for the explosion, but all that happened was a long silence. He didn't even blink for at least sixty seconds. At last he looked down and cleared his throat.

"Let us say grace," said Hector Graybeal.

"Please," said Patty, "if you don't mind, I think Zannah

would like to ask the blessing today. She feels she has a lot to be thankful for."

I nearly fainted. What did she mean? Why hadn't she warned me? My hands started shaking and my mind went blank for what seemed ages. Then I quoted the only thing that came into my head, which was the end of the 121st Psalm.

" 'The Lord shall preserve thy going out and thy coming in from this time forth, and even for evermore.' Thank you, God. Please bless this meal."

All the heads were bowed, but when I looked up I saw Patty's lips curved in a satisfied little 'V' of a smile. Suddenly I understood. Whatever else he said about me, Shem would have a hard time accusing me of witchcraft now. I figured that my going out and my coming in were pretty much guaranteed.

"Amen," I said.

"Amen," said Patty and Hector Graybeal.

"Amen," said Shem.

CHAPTER 7

I KNOW it was very kind of you to bring it," Utopia panted as she worked the dash up and down in the butter churn, "but to be quite truthful it tasted nasty. The taco chips were good and the granola bars were delicious, but no more gum-bubbles, please!"

"Bubble gum," I corrected her. "How could I tell you wouldn't like it? The kids in my class are all crazy about it, so I thought you'd want to try."

Utopia pulled up the wooden dash and examined it closely. "It isn't coming," she said crossly. "I'm sure it's been well over half an hour. The cream must be bewitched."

"You've been working for exactly nineteen minutes," I said, looking at my watch. "Here, let me have a turn."

Utopia wiped her hands on her apron and leaned back against the dairy wall. "It's nasty," she continued. "It's rubbery, and it tastes like medicine, and it sticks to my teeth."

"What does?" I gasped. Churning came harder to me than to the children who had been raised on the dairy.

"Bum-gubbles," said Utopia.

"Bubble gum," I corrected her for the second time. "Suit yourself. How was the peanut butter fudge?"

"The peanut butter fudge," Utopia said, smiling dreamily, "was fabulastic."

"Fabulous," I said, "or fantastic. Not both at once. Hey, what's happening to the cream?"

Utopia inspected the dash again. "What's happening to the cream is butter, silly. See those globs? Here, I'll do it now."

She churned energetically until the fat had collected in a shiny mass, leaving a grayish liquid that Utopia said was buttermilk. Then she taught me to wash the butter and salt it, and form it into fist-sized balls. When the job was done she poured us each a mug of buttermilk.

"There!" she exclaimed, licking the froth from her upper lip. "Isn't that better than Croak?"

"Coke, not Croak," I said, testing my buttermilk suspiciously with the tip of my tongue. "It's all right, I guess. It all depends on what you're used to."

It was chilly in the dairy, but nowhere near as cold as outside. Through the frosted window panes we caught glimpses of bare branches and the pale December sky. The earth had frozen hard, and the duck pond was covered with a layer of ice thick enough for the boys to slide about on safely. I was hoping to do a little sliding myself, once I had finished helping Utopia with her morning chores.

It wasn't the first time I had spent the night at the dairy. Loyal Graybeal had moved up to the attic room on his ninth birthday, leaving the second bed in Utopia's room free for guests. I came whenever I could persuade Mr. Pratt to make an extra trip to the dairy on Friday after school, and stayed until Saturday evening.

I had a little trouble at first from Patty. The bedrooms were unheated in the farmhouse, and she was afraid I'd catch another cold, but I soon convinced her that Utopia and I managed to stay warm in spite of the wintry weather. We wrapped hot bricks in flannel and tucked them under the covers, down by our feet. The bricks lost their warmth before morning, but by then we had made warm nests for ourselves with the feather quilts drawn up around our ears. It was much more fun than sleeping in my own centrally heated bedroom at home, until the time came to get up. Then we would pull on as many clothes as possible under the covers and scoot across the icy floor, downstairs to the kitchen where, with luck, Shem or Hector Graybeal had already started up the wood stove.

Breakfast was the best part of spending the night at the Hunky-Dory Dairy. Mrs. Noah might have no talent for stew, but she was an expert at bacon and griddlecakes and cornmeal mush. She heaped my biscuits with homemade strawberry preserves and let me drink coffee. Obviously no one had ever taught her that it was "bad for growing boys and girls," and I wasn't about to tell her.

The only drawback to breakfast was that you had to get out of bed to have it. Just thinking of it made me shiver.

"If only there were a stove here in the dairy," I said, stamping my feet to shake the numbness out of them. "Why don't you heat this room? It's a wonder the milk doesn't freeze."

"It never has," Utopia said, giving the butter churn one last wipe with a damp rag. "The dairy stays warmer than the bedrooms, you know."

"You should heat the bedrooms, too," I told her crossly. "Not hot like the kitchen, I mean—just warm enough so it isn't torture in the morning. I don't think I could make myself get up for school at all if my room weren't heated."

"You mean there's a stove in your own bedroom at home?" Utopia asked enviously.

"Not a stove, a radiator," I told her. "It's kind of old-fashioned, actually. Most houses have hot air vents nowadays."

Utopia clapped her hands. "Lucky you! I suppose your friendly little devils simply stand there and blow."

"That's right," I said, giggling. "You have to pay them two

dollars an hour and give them beer for breakfast, but they're awfully good at huffing and puffing."

Utopia sighed. "I never know when you're joking, Zannah."

I could hardly blame her. Gradually over the weeks I had been filling her in on life in 1986, and I have to admit that some of the things I described sounded just as outrageous as Utopia's central heating devils. For instance, she liked the idea of Patty's calculator, but computers and what I could remember about silicon chips were too much for her. She was willing to believe that we had made it to the moon and launched a space shuttle, but thought I was joking about television. She approved of vacuum cleaners, Velcro fastenings, and ball-point pens, but when I told her about roller coasters, Water Pics, and video games she burst out laughing.

"However do you dream up those ideas, Zannah?"

"I didn't dream them up," I said. "Inventors did."

"Well, how do *they* dream them up?"

"How should I know? Necessity is the mother of invention," I quoted primly.

"Just what's necessary about a roller coaster?" asked Utopia.

I didn't have a chance to think up a good answer because, looking out the dairy window, we saw Loyal Graybeal take a running leap from the bank of the pond and land with such force that he went clean through the ice.

"Oh, no!" Utopia groaned, hurrying out the door. "I might have known that would happen. He hasn't fallen into a thing for weeks. I began to wonder if he wasn't ailing."

By the time we reached the pond, Loyal had rescued himself with the help of the younger Noahs and a fallen branch, but the pond was ruined for sliding. The boys were chilled to the bone, so we coaxed Hector Graybeal to build a fire in the parlor, and we all cooked apples on roasting forks over the embers.

The apples had been stored in a cool, dark room in the cellar. Their skins were wrinkled, but the fruit inside was sweeter than when it was fresh from the tree. Hot and slightly charred, it was delicious. I ate two and Shem had four, one on top of another, before he called it "baby food" and scornfully left the room.

"He seems more sociable than usual though," I observed. "Who knows, we may end up friends!"

Utopia shook her head. "Don't get your hopes up. Shem has a poor opinion of women folk. Except for his mother, that is. He thinks she's downright perfect."

"Well, she's not too bad," I admitted. "Especially since Patty showed her how to do her hair."

It was true that Mrs. Noah looked better. In fact she looked happier, too. Instead of wilting over the kitchen stove, she bustled about cheerfully, singing snatches of hymns, and joking, and even giving Hector Graybeal a little sass if he bossed her around too much. She was the perfect illustration of Patty's theory that there's nothing like washing your hair for lifting your spirits. Not that it was just a question of hair—she looked better all over.

"She kind of spoils the effect with those awful boots, though," I told Utopia.

Since the start of the cold weather, Mrs. Noah had taken to wearing a pair of old leather boots. They were scratched and worn, a little moldy around the stitching, and several sizes too big for her.

"They're Father's," Utopia explained. "They're all she has to wear, winter *or* summer. When we were removed from the big farm she was wearing slippers, and they wore out long ago. That's why she goes barefoot most of the year."

"At least she stays the same size," I said. "What do you and the boys do when your feet grow bigger?"

Utopia looked down at her feet. "These are Shem's," she said ruefully. "Shem moved into another pair of Father's. Luckily Father never threw away his old boots—waste not, want not, he says—but I'm afraid we all want new boots all the same. Poor Loyal is wearing an old pair of my mother's. She had tiny feet. Don't tease him about them! Not that you can tell they're a woman's boots anymore. He slathers them with mud to disguise them. We're all wearing hand-me-downs except for Father."

I thought it would be a simple matter for Mr. Pratt to bring new boots from town, but when I suggested it on my way home that day, he sighed and rubbed his chin.

"Leather boots cost money, Zannah. It would run to several hundred dollars to outfit the lot of them, and even back in *their* time, leather boots couldn't be had for milk, butter, and eggs."

"We could manage somehow among the three of us," I argued. "Patty and I could have a garage sale or something to raise the money."

Mr. Pratt looked doubtful. "They're proud people. I don't see Hector accepting charity."

I groaned with frustration. "It kills me—just think of all the things we have in our lives that would make their lives easier! But we can't bring them to the dairy because they think it's either charity or witchcraft. Why did I ever get mixed up with these people?"

It wasn't until the next morning at breakfast that I thought of a solution. "Why leather?" I wondered.

One of the nice things about Patty is that she doesn't think you're crazy when you say something like that out of the blue. She just waits patiently for you to explain.

"Why leather boots? Why not *rubber* boots?" I asked.

Patty laughed. "I can just see them—all seven of them waddling around in rubber boots like a family of puddle-ducks."

"You wouldn't laugh if you could see Utopia's feet," I said reprovingly. "They're covered with blisters. She isn't really Shem's size, you know. She wears these awful socks inside that Mrs. Noah knits, all knots and bumps, and they don't help, believe me."

"Poor baby!" said Patty, sobering up. "I think rubber boots might be just the ticket. They wouldn't cost too much, and we could put in some woolly inner soles to warm them up. But how do we find out their sizes?"

It remained a problem until I noticed some artwork that the Tinies had taped up on the wall. It looked like giant flowers, only the petals were in the shapes of hands and feet.

"How did you do that?" I asked.

"We took our shoes off and traced around our socks," said Patty. "Some of them are hands, of course. Didn't you see the handprint turkeys we did for Thanksgiving? You make a head out of the thumb, and the fingers are—" When Patty starts in on her art projects she's capable of talking nonstop for as much as an hour.

I cut her short. "I saw them. Thanks! You just gave me an idea."

The next time I went to the dairy, I brought some sheets of red and green construction paper and a pair of scissors. Under the pretext of making giant poinsettia blossoms to decorate the walls for Christmas, I persuaded everyone but Hector Graybeal to trace around their socks. Hector Graybeal refused to remove his boots. I had to trace around the outside, so some of the petals were twice as big as all the rest. The result looked pretty silly on the kitchen wall, but no one at the dairy had ever seen a poinsettia anyway, so I got away with it. By evening I had made copies of everybody's footprints to take back home to Patty.

The salesman probably thought we were crazy when we asked for seven pairs of rubber boots, all different sizes. He kept saying that you couldn't fit a person right, just comparing the soles with a bunch of footprints. I finally said we had to do it that way because the people we were buying the boots for couldn't leave their house.

He was a little skeptical. "All seven of them?"

I nodded firmly. "All seven."

"Then why do they need boots?" he asked.

The shoe store had been ten miles from the city, in the kind of mall that looks like an airplane hangar, where you can buy things for half price. The ride home got my spirits down: everything you could see from the highway was dull and ugly, and you could tell that more of the same was being built up fast. We passed three more shopping malls, two of them still under construction, and a handful of bowling alleys, and about a million fast-food restaurants. The one time we drove by a leftover scrap of farm with some scruffy cows staring over a fence at the highway, it looked depressing and completely out of place.

"Think how they'd hate it!" I said, meaning the families at the dairy.

Patty agreed. "Spreading suburbia. It sounds like a disease and if you ask me, it looks like one, too. It's a good thing those poor people can't come out for a glimpse of the twentieth century. They'd get the shock of their lives."

"I'd give up the twentieth century like a shot if I had a chance," I told her. "Patty, *really*, wouldn't it be wonderful if we could move in with them? Just think—a lifetime of nice people and fresh air! You're always saying how we should get back to basics and lead a simpler life and all that. Why don't we just do it?"

Patty sighed. "I don't know, Zannah. It's a temptation, for sure, but I don't think you can turn your back on your own time and place. Not once you've known it. Living at the dairy would be like playing house."

"Well, why not?" I asked, scowling out the window at a cluster of gas stations. "Why not play? Why should life be all hard work?"

"Good question," said Patty, "but the answer isn't the Hunky-Dory Dairy. When I said 'playing house' I didn't mean no hard work. I meant we'd be pretending all the time, because we know how modern life can be. But we'd be working our asses off all the same, believe me!"

I blushed. "Patty!"

"Sorry," she said, "but don't kid yourself. It's not just the wood stove and the outhouse and having no washer and dryer I'd worry about. It's serious things, like living without modern medicine. What happens if one of them gets really sick?"

We soon found out.

When we arrived home from the shoe store, I telephoned to Mr. Pratt at his office. "It's Friday," I reminded him. "How about driving me out to the dairy when you get back from work?"

Mr. Pratt groaned. "Again? You've stayed there three weekends in a row."

"Not the whole weekend," I said. "Just Friday night. Patty and I bought the boots today, so it's really important. Please? Pretty please with sugar on it?"

"How about pretty please with milk, butter, and eggs?" asked Mr. Pratt.

I laughed. "All right, pretty please with *scrambled* eggs. See you after work today, okay? And hurry! I'll get Patty to fix you a snack, if you're good."

"Perfect little hostess," Mr. Pratt said sarcastically. "My time is precious, you know. Not that you care."

But he must have been looking for an excuse to leave work, because he arrived at our door exactly twenty-seven minutes after I hung up the phone.

Patty lined up the boots in the back of the van and handed Mr. Pratt a cold beer. "You get the snack when you come back from the dairy," she told him. "I made lasagna for dinner and I need someone to eat up Zannah's share. You're free, I hope."

"Free as a bird!" Mr. Pratt said cheerfully, giving a little flick of the reins to start up the mare.

"Oh, and Zannah!" Patty called after me. "Wear your turtleneck to bed. Wear your socks, too, okay? No running around barefoot on those floors. Promise?"

"That's her mother hen act," I explained to Mr. Pratt. "Most of the time she forgets it, so when she remembers, she lays it on twice as thick. But Utopia and the other kids have been living at the dairy for years, and they *never* get colds."

Night was falling by the time we reached the farm, and as we trotted across the meadow we could see the parlor windows swollen with light.

"That's funny! Graybeal doesn't usually hold with putting out so many lamps," said Mr. Pratt. "If they knew anyone besides us and your mother, I'd say they were having a party."

It was hardly a party. Mrs. Noah met us at the door, her face pale with worry. All traces of her new hairstyle had disappeared, and her clothes looked as if she had thrown them on backwards.

"Oh, dear," she sighed. "I'm afraid you won't get much entertainment here tonight. Not that we aren't always pleased to see Zannah, but Japheth isn't well at all!"

While Mr. Pratt was pressing for details I pushed past her into the kitchen and ran up to Utopia, who was lifting a steaming kettle off the stove. "What happened? Where's Japheth?"

"In the parlor," said Utopia. "Father made a bed for him there, so as to be close to the fire. It's so cold over the dairy, and we don't have your friendly devils to huff and puff."

"Don't be silly," I said. "What's wrong with Japheth?"

Utopia poured a mugful of a foul-smelling liquid. "Oh, Zannah, I'm so worried! We all get colds from time to time, but nothing has ever been so bad as this. He's terribly hot to touch, but he shivers and says he's freezing. When he makes sense at all, that is. Mostly he talks complete nonsense. Come and see for yourself."

I felt a little guilty, remembering my confidence when I told Mr. Pratt that no one caught colds at the dairy. I also felt more than a little curious. Had they invented thermometers a hundred years ago? Did they have aspirin? And what was in the mug that Utopia had filled for Japheth? Anything that smelled so horrible must be close to impossible to swallow.

Mrs. Noah bustled past me into the parlor, followed by Mr. Pratt. "Let me have that, Utopia. Did you remember to sweeten it? Oh, dear, he looks so feverish! Sit up, Japheth, and try to swallow this. But keep the blanket right up to your chin, mind!"

Japheth did not sit up. I don't think he heard what his mother was saying, or at least he didn't understand. His cheek was burning hot when I touched it, and there were tears running out of his eyes. Not the kind of tears you cry from being angry or hurt or sad; the kind you cry without even knowing it.

"Gosh!" I said. "He's *really* sick, isn't he! What's his temperature?"

Mrs. Noah looked at me uncomprehendingly.

Suddenly my whole body tingled with impatience. "Why are you keeping him so hot?" I asked. "That's no way to bring his fever down. When a little kid gets that high a temperature it can be dangerous! You should put him in a cool tub, or at least wrap him in wet towels."

"Wet towels!" Mrs. Noah exclaimed in a shocked voice. "Do you want to kill him?"

I felt like screaming. "I want to get his temperature down, is all. What's that you're trying to make him drink?"

"It's an infusion," Mrs. Noah said as she struggled to prop Japheth up and spoon a little of the liquid between his lips. "It's quite effective, if only he would take it. There's pepper and sassafras and oil of nutmeg—oh, what a waste!"

Sick as he was, Japheth had summoned the strength to spit out his mother's brew.

Mrs. Noah wrinkled her brow and looked in dismay at the widening stains on the sheet. "Oil of nutmeg is so very dear!" she explained sadly.

"Let's just hope it works," I said, picking up a large glass bottle from the table near Japheth's bed. "What's this stuff?"

"Tonic," said Mrs. Noah. She lowered Japheth back on his pillow and pulled the blankets up around his ears until I couldn't see more than two square inches of his face.

"Tonic?" I repeated. "That's what Patty mixes with gin."

I read the label and it might well have been gin, from all it said in the description: "Miraculous remedy possessing inimitable powers of clearing the lungs, purging the digestive parts, reinforcing the walls of the stomach, purifying the complexion, and fortifying the blood." There was no mention of ingredients.

I pulled out the stopper and sniffed. "Yuck! How much of this does Japheth have to take?"

"I'm sure the more he takes the faster he'll be cured," said Mrs. Noah. "Unfortunately he rejects it. Poor, misguided child! He's too young to understand that it's for his own good."

"That might be just as well," I said. "Japheth, where does it hurt? Is it your throat? Do you have a tummy-ache?"

Japheth looked right through me. For a minute I was afraid he had become a nuisance and we wouldn't be able to see each other anymore. Then suddenly I forgot about the magic and was really scared.

"Mrs. Noah, he's awfully sick, you know. No joke! I don't think any of this stuff is going to help, even if he *does* take it. I think he needs a doctor."

A deep voice rumbled behind me. I spun around and saw Hector Graybeal, scowling so ferociously that I would have thought he was mad at me if I didn't know that he was just as scared as the rest of us.

"There is no doctoring to be had in these parts," he said. "You know we can't leave our land, and no one but yourselves has ever been able to come in. We can only do our best with what we have on hand and pray for the Lord's mercy."

"Praying is all very well," I said crossly, "but it can be helped along with antibiotics."

The word had slipped out in spite of me. I knew it was unwise to mention modern drugs, but it gave me an idea. "Patty's a nurse!" I said excitedly. "She'll know what to do."

Patty was astonished when I reappeared on the doorstep with Mr. Pratt. "Back already? Both of you? What made you change your mind, Zannah?"

When I had explained she moaned and shook her head. "I knew that would happen sooner or later. I just *knew* it! What has Marigold been doing for him?"

I described the foul-smelling brew and the label on the bottle of tonic. "They hadn't even taken his temperature!" I told her angrily. "I don't think they own a thermometer. What do you suppose that tonic was? Some old-fashioned kind of penicillin?"

"Penicillin wasn't invented until 1928," said Patty, "and they didn't really use it on people until the forties. They didn't have much use for medical thermometers a hundred years ago, either. Oh, dear, I don't know what to say! I suppose the herb tea won't do him any harm, but I'm worried about the tonic. Those old quack remedies were full of opiates. I just hope she didn't give him too much."

"He's a smart kid. He spits everything out," I said. "Oh, come on, Patty! We've got to help him. Can't you just grab some antibiotics and come back to the dairy with us? He's really sick! He might die while we're standing here talking."

Patty sighed. "I don't keep antibiotics lying around, and I'm not qualified to prescribe any. Even if I could, how do I know what he needs? For all I know he has pneumonia, or appendicitis, or diphtheria, or—"

Mr. Pratt put his arm around her shoulders. "Calm down," he said. "He isn't going to die before you get there, but he really needs you. I'd say it was flu, personally. Maybe strep throat. I'm no expert. But you're the only one who can help. How about it?"

Patty threw everything she could think of into a suitcase: aspirin and a hot water bottle and some Vicks Vaporub and a bottle of the syrup she gives me when I have a cold. She even got a doctor friend of hers to phone a prescription to the pharmacy, and when we stopped by to pick it up she bought a whole lot of other stuff, too.

It turned out we didn't need most of it. Japheth had some kind of virus, with a sore throat and swollen glands—the kind the kids and I keep getting at school. In fact, Patty said I probably carried it to him from the twentieth century. She gave him the antibiotic and some aspirin for the fever, and wrote down on a piece of paper how long he should go on taking everything. By the time we started home again, Japheth's temperature had gone down to 101°.

"How did you get away with giving him all that modern stuff?" I asked on my way home.

I was feeling pretty sleepy; it was almost midnight. Mr. Pratt had pulled an old blanket out of the back of the van, and the three of us huddled under it as the mare trudged through the cold streets of Burleith.

Patty sounded embarrassed. "I have to admit I was a little underhanded. I never let them see the thermometer, and when Hector asked about the antibiotic I told him it was an herbal recipe I inherited from my grandmother."

I laughed. "Granny Marie Curie, for instance?"

"Someone like that." Patty gave me a hug. "See what I mean about living in our own century? I won't say Japheth owes his life to people like her—not this time—but I wouldn't have wanted to take any chances. I'm getting too fond of the Hunky-Dory Dairy!"

The Georgetown University bells rang twelve strokes for midnight. I closed my eyes and pretended they were wedding bells, ringing for Hector Graybeal and my mother.

CHAPTER 8

JAPHETH WAS UP and around by Christmas, and none the worse for the wear. He had a nasty cough for a while, but Mrs. Noah dosed him regularly with a mixture of honey and blackberry wine. When Patty tasted it, she said it beat any of the commercial cough syrups she had tried on me.

Japheth's bed was moved back to his room over the dairy, and the parlor became once again the dark and formal place I had known it, with its curtains drawn and its scratchy horsehair sofa protected from dust by a linen sheet. Japheth, however, having supposedly been at death's door, was spoiled rotten and acted too big for his boots for weeks to come.

Talking of boots, the ones Patty and I bought at the discount store were received with great enthusiasm. Everyone at the dairy, from Japheth up to Hector Graybeal, wore them nonstop for the rest of the winter. As Patty had tucked in store-bought knee socks for the children, Utopia's feet were back to normal.

In fact the boots were such a success that our Christmas presents for the dairy were an anticlimax by comparison. We gave Utopia *Rebecca of Sunnybrook Farm*, Mrs. Noah a Teflon frying pan, Hector Graybeal a monkey wrench, and each of the boys a Swiss army knife. But nothing was quite as popular as the rubber boots.

When it came right down to it, the ones most impressed by their Christmas presents were me and Patty.

"It's so touching!" said Patty, holding up a square of needlework that spelled out GOD BLESS THIS HOME. "Marigold, of all people! She simply *despises* anything that involves holding a needle. Think of the time she spent— I'm going to frame it!"

"I'd frame *this* if I could, but I think Utopia's feelings would be hurt if I didn't wear it," I said, winding a lumpy gray wool scarf around my neck.

Patty's eyes sparkled with mischief. "Very elegant—Utopia should patent it for victims of whiplash. What was in the other package?"

I hesitated. The other package had contained something far more precious than the scarf, but I hardly dared believe that it was a token of friendship. What if some trick were involved?

"Come look." Cupped in my hands was a perfect, tiny bird's nest.

"How sweet!" said Patty. "Is that from Utopia?"

"No," I said. "It's from Shem."

Shem had changed, but in a way I couldn't understand. Since his brother's illness he treated Patty with new respect and me with something like affection, but when I tried to talk to him and show I wanted to be friends, he would say something rude and slip away. It was as if he liked me yet didn't like me, enjoyed my company, yet would rather I weren't there.

The bird's nest was proof. When I thanked him, he first blushed and then shouted, "Don't think it means anything, Zannah!"

I put the nest on a shelf over my bed—the very highest shelf, because in little more than a week, the house would once more be invaded by the Tiny Fingers Preschool Playgroup.

The new basement-playroom was ready for the reopening of school on the fifth of January. Patty, Mr. Pratt, and I worked hard all vacation, scrubbing, and cleaning, and polishing the big, high windows. Even though it was mostly underground, it seemed brighter than the upstairs rooms. The walls were pale yellow, there were mirrors everywhere, and Mr. Pratt had revealed a secret talent by painting a mural with life-sized baby animals. There was almost no furniture because Patty maintained that the Tinies always ended up on the floor, but there were lots of shelves and big wicker baskets for putting things away.

"It's fabulastic!" I told Patty, borrowing Utopia's new word. "Once the parents see this, everybody in town will be sending their kids to you."

"Only twenty-four," Patty said firmly. "That's all I can manage until I get my full-time assistant. Then we'll see."

"Who's your assistant going to be?" I asked. "I wouldn't count on Lafayette if I were you."

In spite of her hopes, Lafayette's baby wasn't born on Christmas Day. It came a week later, just as all the bells and sirens went off on New Year's Eve.

Lafayette was disappointed until she discovered that her son was the first child to be born in Washington, D.C., in 1987. There was a big picture of her with the baby in the "Metro" section of the *Washington Post*, and she got a lot of coupons and free baby clothes and things.

"And Washington is the capital of the United States," she crowed when she came to show off her baby, "so he's like the first American baby of 1987!"

I didn't quite follow her reasoning. Chances were that some kid was born a few seconds earlier, in some place like Salt Lake City, but I didn't want to spoil her fun. I was a little shocked, though, when Lafayette told me what she had named him.

"Acme?" I repeated. "What kind of weird name is that? It sounds like a skin disease!"

"It means 'tops,' " Lafayette told me. "Like, *the* best. It gives a kid confidence to have a name that shows what his parents think of him. After all, everything else is against him in this crazy world."

"Starting with his birthday," I said pessimistically. "He may have made it past December 25, but he's still going to get presents that say 'Merry Christmas and happy birthday' all the rest of his life. There ought to be a law to protect kids like us."

My own birthday isn't on any spectacular date like Christmas or New Year's; it's the sixth of January. Even when people remember, which they usually don't, they're too bankrupt or hung over to do anything about it. When I was little, Patty used to throw a half-birthday party for me in July, but as I grew older it seemed too babyish. I wasn't expecting much on my twelfth birthday, so I was really overwhelmed when I came down to breakfast to find Mr. Pratt waiting for me with a heap of presents.

Patty was squeezing grapefruit juice, but when she saw me she stopped the machine and started singing instead. "Happy birthday to you! You live in a zoo—"

I giggled. "That's an understatement. You should call it the 'Tiny *Paws* Preschool Playgroup.' I hope being twelve rates something special for breakfast. How about French toast?"

"How about birthday cake?" asked Mr. Pratt. He turned his back, fumbled with a cigarette lighter, and swung around, holding a three-layer spice cake with butterscotch frosting.

I made an unsuccessful effort not to drool. "Cake for breakfast?" I asked, a little shocked.

"I blush to admit it," said Patty. "Peter tells me you've developed a taste for coffee, too. Eat, drink, and be merry, and don't tell the school nutritionist."

It turned out the cake was from Mrs. Noah, who maybe for the first time in her life forgot to mistake salt for sugar, or slam the oven door just when the batter began to rise. There were other presents, too: clumsy wooden figures whittled by the three little boys, a nubbly hat from Utopia to match my knitted scarf, and last, wrapped in a scrap of rag and tied with a string, three smooth, shiny pebbles shaped like eggs, to fit inside my nest.

"I don't understand Shem," I said to myself as I tucked the pebbles into the nest before leaving for school that morning. "If he likes me enough for presents, why does he keep telling me to stay away?"

When I hopped out of the van and thanked him on Friday evening, he was just the same. First he turned red and his eyes crinkled in what might have been a smile. Then he kicked the frozen earth with the toe of a rubber boot that looked as though it had done so much kicking, it might not last the winter.

"Better think again if you're fixing to stay with us tonight," he said gruffly. "There'll be snow by morning. No weather for softies like you and your mother."

"My mother isn't here, and I'm no softy," I answered. "I'm as tough as you are, and I'll prove it if you try to boss me around, Shem Rudge."

Then I laughed. It seemed a funny way to be thanking him for his present. "If it snows, let's hope there's a lot of it," I said. "That slope down to your pond would be perfect for sledding."

Shem turned away sullenly, and I ran into the kitchen. I had brought something so daring out of the twentieth century to show off to Utopia that my heart was pounding with excitement. For my birthday Patty had given me a transistor radio small enough to fit in the palm of my hand. I wasn't sure it would work at the dairy and if it did, my conscience told me that it might not be wise to use it, but the temptation was too great to resist.

Utopia was helping Mrs. Noah to prepare cream cheese. I watched carefully as they poured the heavy cream into shallow wooden boxes lined with cloth and arranged the boxes on a rack where the air could circulate. I wanted to know how to do everything myself by the time I was a permanent member of the dairy.

"How long until it's ready?" I asked.

"A day or so," said Utopia. "There's no hurry—we haven't finished eating the last batch."

"If it weren't such a waste of money I'd bring you some supermarket cream cheese," I said when Mrs. Noah left the room. "You wouldn't believe how fake it tastes compared with this. When we come to live here, I'll never have to eat store-bought food again."

For the first time, Utopia looked doubtful. "I don't see how you can move to the farm now that your mother has started her big new school. She'll never want to leave."

I sighed. "I know. I've been worrying about it. But I suppose she could find someone to take it over. After all, she says there's a full-time assistant coming to help her. I just wish your father would hurry up and propose. They say love conquers all!"

Utopia wrung out a rag and hung it up to dry. "What did you bring this time?" she asked eagerly.

I pulled some envelopes of Kool-Aid out of my pocket. "You mix this with water. I bet you like it! I brought some other stuff, too, only not to eat. Patty gave me a whole pile of old workbooks to teach the boys with, and there's a blackboard in the back of the van. It's kind of old-fashioned, but you can still write on it."

Utopia laughed. It always amused her to hear me say *old-fashioned.* "Old-fashioned just for you, or for both of us?"

"I don't know," I admitted. "In Washington schools, blackboards are green nowadays. Come and see!"

When Utopia saw the blackboard she laughed again and said it was only a slate, but she was glad to have it. "Now we can do sums without begging Father for paper," she said. "Be sure to thank your mother, Zannah. Is that all?"

She sounded like one of the little kids I baby-sit for, who pesters his mother for a present every time she goes out and comes home again.

"Isn't that enough?" I teased. "There's one more thing, though. Something unbelievable—you're not going to believe your ears!"

I was beginning to enjoy modern inventions as much as Utopia. Seen all over again through her eyes, they seemed wild and daring, each one a sort of miracle. And since she was the only member of the dairy who showed any curiosity for the world I came from, I took advantage of her.

We slipped across the moonlit barnyard, into the dark shelter of the barn, past the heavily breathing cows that exuded warmth like living islands. Up in our secret room, it was so cold that my fingers could hardly turn the radio dial, but after a lot of squeaks and static I finally tuned in on Q107.

"That's this fantastic group called 'Heat Rash,' " I told Utopia. "They're singing 'Credit Risk.' You can't always get the words because of the weird sound effects, but believe me, it's fabulastic! It was a top hit for ages."

Utopia leaned forward eagerly, her eyes shining with appreciation.

"Listen, it's really neat!" I tapped my foot and joined in whenever I remembered the words. " 'Bug off, friend—I'll tell you why—Your card expired—in July—' "

Utopia looked bewildered. "Tell them to sing louder!"

I stared at her. "Huh? Tell who?"

"The friendly devils in the box," she said.

We listened to a few more songs before I slipped the transistor back into the pocket of my down jacket. "It's getting late," I said. "Besides, it's creepy here at night. I keep hearing all these noises. Are you sure no one knows about this place? I wouldn't want to get you in trouble."

Gripping my elbow, Utopia guided me through the hayloft. "Just cats," she reassured me. "Owls and cats."

When we came out into the barnyard we could no longer see the moon. The snow was falling thick and fast.

In wintertime it was always dark when we woke up at the dairy. I ought not to have minded because we went to bed early, too, but all the same, I hated the sound of logs being tossed into the wood stove and heavy boots tramping out to the barn, because they meant I would have to crawl out from under my warm, feather quilt.

That Saturday I heard the rattle and thump of logs tumbling over last night's coals, and the slow creak of the kitchen door opening, but no boots. There was a strange hush about the morning, and although it was still dark, it was a paler kind of dark than usual. Then I heard Shem and Hector Graybeal talking outside. Without the accompanying sound of footsteps, it was as if their voices were floating over the barnyard.

"Clear a path—" I heard one of them saying as the voices drew closer to the house. "Fetch a shovel—"

I swung my legs over the side of the bed, walked to the window, and looked out. The world of the Hunky-Dory Dairy was blanketed with snow.

Utopia's chores that morning seemed to drag on endlessly. Together we aired the beds, swept the kitchen floor, washed and put away the breakfast dishes, and peeled potatoes for lunch. Muffling ourselves in bulky shawls, scarves, and mittens we waded out to the dairy to ladle off the cream that had risen to the top of the cans after last night's milking, and we carried the skim milk left over to the barn for the animals. Then, although it was ordinarily Shem's job, we helped the little boys to clean the box stalls and spread fresh hay. Shem had more important work to do that morning. I could see his breath rising in pale clouds as he puffed and grunted over his snowshovel.

Up in our secret room, it was so cold that my fingers could hardly turn the radio dial, but after a lot of squeaks and static I finally tuned in on Q107.

"There!" Utopia gasped triumphantly as she leaned the pitch-fork against a wall. "We're free—and a good two hours before we have to help with lunch."

The little boys had finished, too, and appeared in an expectant trio, all three bundled up until they looked as fat as they were tall. The earflaps of their woolen caps were pulled down to meet their turned-up collars, and both flaps and collars were wrapped about with scarves. All that I could see of skin was the tips of their moist, pink noses.

"Quick!" said Loyal. "Where are the sleds?"

We found two sleds in the feed room and a toboggan propped in a corner of the calves' shed, shrouded in cobwebs; the last big snow had been two years before. Dragging them behind us, we trudged through knee-deep snow toward the back of the barn and the steep slope to the pond.

"But where's the pond?" asked Ham. "It disappeared!"

Even the ice was covered, although you could make out where it was by a round depression in the snow.

Sleds turned out to be useless. The snow was so fresh and powdery that instead of packing it into slippery tracks, the runners cut through to the earth below. But the toboggan flattened a narrow runway, and with each trip we sped down faster. First Loyal went, with Japheth lying on his back. Then I had a turn with Ham, and last of all Utopia and I went together. The two of us made a wobbly, top-heavy load, and halfway down the slope we veered to the side and tumbled face-first into the snow. Our cheeks burned but we shrieked with laughter as we slithered our way back uphill and handed the toboggan to Loyal for his second turn.

"Fabulastic!" screamed Utopia on our sixth trip down. "I wish the snow would last forever!"

But Washington winters are too warm for snow to stay long on the ground. Already it was sinking, packing together, changing from fluff to icy clay that clung to our mittens. Soon our runway was streaked with the dirt that we dug loose with our heels as we tramped again and again up the hill.

The little boys began to whimper. "My wrists hurt!" said Japheth, tearfully staring at the expanse of red skin between his wet cuffs and his wet mittens.

Ham and Loyal had so much snow packed into the tops of their boots that their legs reminded me of the bottle of champagne I had prepared for Patty's birthday, months before, gleamingly dark in its nest of ice.

Utopia became maternal. "Home for all of you!" she declared, warming her fingers against her flushed cheeks. "Run along, Loyal! Zannah and I will put the sleds away. You take Ham and Japheth back to the kitchen. Hang up the mittens by the stove, but mind you leave your boots outside."

She grabbed a sled rope in each hand and turned impatiently to see if I was following with the toboggan, but I hung behind.

"Just one more time!" I begged. "You live here, but I go home this afternoon."

"Suit yourself," said Utopia. "I have to feed the hens before I set the table."

I promised myself to stop after one more ride, but I couldn't resist seeing how the toboggan performed with a lighter load. Taking a running start from the top of the slope, I shot forward and braced myself for the wild swoop down to the pond. So far we had always stopped a few feet from the bank. With a lightened load, would the toboggan go any farther?

I never found out. A moment after I had flung myself down, someone leapt on top of me, gripping my shoulders as the toboggan heaved dangerously from side to side. I screamed and was unable to catch my breath again, with the weight pressing from above.

"Hold on!" shouted Shem. "How's that for speed?"

We hurtled down the slope, gained speed as we struck the ice, hit the far bank of the pond with a terrifying jerk, and collapsed in a jumble of arms and legs.

I was too weak to protest. The toboggan had landed upside down on top of me, and when Shem removed it I was more thankful than angry.

"You brute!" I gasped, laughing shakily. "Couldn't you warn me? It felt like a wild bull on the rampage."

Shem snorted; he had snow up his nostrils. "Sorry, Zannah," he grunted as he pried more snow loose from his collar. "But it was worth it."

I couldn't think of a word to say, following Shem back through the melting snow. Unless I was mistaken, he had apologized, but I wasn't even sure he had much to apologize for. In fact, I felt flattered. He took the toboggan back to the barn and actually smiled at me when he slid into his place at the lunch table, only just on time to hear Hector Graybeal ask the blessing.

When Mr. Pratt came by to pick me up, the wheels of the van skidding giddily behind the mare, I was waiting on the kitchen step, sucking an icicle. I felt puffed up with satisfaction. My fingers ached, my cheeks were scorched, and my legs felt like Jell-O, but it had been a glorious day and I had made friends with the only person who didn't want me at the dairy.

Utopia was inside giving the younger Noahs their Saturday night bath, but Shem hung around to see me off. Slouching a little, his hands thrust in his pockets, he squinted at me and gave a friendly shrug as Mr. Pratt turned the mare toward home.

My happiness was complete until I heard him singing behind us in the snowy twilight, a tuneless but recognizable song: " 'Bug off, friend—I'll tell you why—' "

There was only one time, one place where Shem could have

heard that song. What else had he heard? How long had that rat
been listening? In a split second, my heart hit rock bottom. If
Shem knew all our plans he'd be sure to make trouble one way
or another. Or would he? Was he on my side now, or was he
just pretending?

CHAPTER 9

To my astonishment, Lafayette returned to work at the Tiny Fingers Preschool Playgroup when Acme was only one month old. The new assistant hadn't shown up yet, and Patty was acting a little more frazzled than usual, so I was grateful. The only drawback was that Acme came, too. Lafayette wore him in a kind of sling around her waist, and when he wasn't asleep he glared out at the Tinies, his beady little eyes glinting in his cross little face.

When I asked Lafayette what he was so mad about, she said he had every right to be mad, being born into this sick, self-destructive world of ours.

"We're destroying our resources," she told me. "What'll be left for him by the time he's my age? Garbage, that's all. Fallout and garbage. But what do we care? We won't be around to suffer the consequences."

I knew for a fact that Lafayette was twenty-four. If she didn't plan to be around when Acme was her age, it meant she would die before she was fifty. Unless she was counting on retiring to a condominium on the moon. I didn't ask her to explain, however, because nowadays Lafayette talked in a blue streak every time you asked her a question, and it was always this gloomy stuff about the awful world Acme was born into.

Lafayette didn't look as gloomy as she sounded. In fact, in

all the time I had known her, I had never seen her so bright and active. She moved much faster: whisking around the basement-playroom, picking up a toy here, tying a shoelace there, wiping noses all over the place. I have to admit she was a help to Patty, except for her crazy new ideas about nutrition.

Back in the old days when Lafayette was slow and soothing, her lunch would be something like a diet soda and a package of Hostess Twinkies. But ever since Acme was born, she started cramming our refrigerator full of bean sprouts, and rutabaga bread, and soy substitutes for foods I didn't know existed to be substituted for. She nearly killed me one day when she discovered I had thrown out something that looked and smelled like spoiled milk. Apparently it was clabber. When I looked it up in the dictionary it seemed to me clabber *was* spoiled milk, but Lafayette said that when you spoil milk on purpose it's nutritious, so you don't throw it out.

"Why don't you just drink *fresh* milk?" I asked, after apologizing as sincerely as I was able.

"Because it's poison, that's why," said Lafayette. "The cows have poison in their systems from all the DDT, and there's poison in the food they eat, so what can you expect? You think I want to poison Acme, too?"

I was shocked. "You're not feeding *him* clabber, are you?"

"I'm nursing him," Lafayette explained. "Anything I eat or drink enters my system and goes right through to him. That's why I have to stay pure."

Judging by the look and smell of what Lafayette kept in our refrigerator, Acme was a tough little kid. He'd have to be, the way his system put up with all the weird stuff in his mother's system.

"There isn't any poison in our milk," I told Lafayette confidently. "Or the eggs or the butter, either. They come from this farm where everything's natural."

"Oh, yeah? said Lafayette. "Nothing's natural these days. What about radioactivity? What about acid rain?"

"There wasn't any acid rain a hundred years ago," I said unthinkingly.

Lafayette stared. "You're trying to tell me you drink century-old milk?"

"Well, not exactly—" I began.

"Forget it," she said, interrupting me. "I'll settle for clabber."

It wouldn't have mattered if Lafayette had confined her new eating habits to herself and Acme, but unfortunately she couldn't resist practicing on the Tinies as well. When some poor kid pulled a peanut butter and jelly sandwich out of his lunchbox, Lafayette would wheedle it away from him and give him prune butter and sprouts on rice cakes instead.

This didn't go over too well with the Tinies, and we began getting nasty notes from some of the parents. Patty was able to bluff her way out of it by making up some story about adventures with nutrition; parents tend to feel a little guilty when you mention the word *nutrition*. But she had to be a little firm with Lafayette, and Lafayette became worse than ever about the self-destruction of the modern world.

"Face the facts, Patty," I said one evening after an outraged father had called up to complain that Lafayette had given his little girl nightmares, telling her chocolate milk was poison. "Lafayette is more trouble than she's worth."

"She's a terrific help!" Patty protested. "She used to be so slow, and half the time she didn't even turn up. Now she never misses a day, and she really pulls the place together."

"Want to know why she never misses a day?" I asked. "Because she doesn't want to miss a meal, that's why. She keeps all her food in our refrigerator. You do all her laundry for her, too, admit it."

"Not all of it," said Patty, "but why shouldn't I help out? It's no trouble. I just toss it in with ours."

I exploded. "You marshmallow! I'm the one who folds the wash, remember? Yesterday there were twenty-seven diapers and three white socks. One of the socks must have been hers; I never saw it before. Why should you be paying her a salary just so you can wash her clothes?"

"You're exaggerating," said Patty.

"*She's* exaggerating," I argued. "Hasn't she ever heard of disposable diapers?"

"Pollution," Patty said automatically. "Squandering the earth's resources—"

"Sure," I said. "She doesn't want to throw out a Pamper, so instead you wear out our machine, run up our electricity bill, and waste your time and mine. Time is money, right? I bet if I figure out the time and power we use and all that, *we'd* be the ones squandering the earth's resources. Where's your calculator?"

Patty burst out laughing and collapsed into an armchair. "Forget it, you're probably right. As a matter of fact, today was Lafayette's last day—she's got some kind of job working on a health food farm, starting next week. She says it'll be a better life for Acme. But don't worry, I have a plan. Everything's going to be hunky-dory, like Peter says. Listen, honey—I promised not to say anything until Sunday, but believe me, I have the most fantastic good news!"

"Oh!" I said. I looked at her twinkling eyes and the proud little smile on her face. "Oh, Patty! Is it what I think it is?"

Patty blushed. "How can I tell what you've been thinking? You'll find out on Sunday."

That was Friday night. I couldn't get hold of Mr. Pratt to drive me to the dairy, but I went out with him early Saturday morning. For the first time ever, I was impatient with the mare.

I had such beautiful news—such important news!—and the poor old thing would hardly keep up her trot for two minutes at a time before lapsing into a lazy amble.

"What's up, Zannah?" Mr. Pratt asked after a while. "You look as if you just inherited a million dollars."

"I just inherited the whole world!" I told him, and my voice kept catching, I was so excited. "At least, the only part of it I ever wanted."

"Can you let me in on the secret?" he asked.

"I'm afraid not," I said. "I'd love to, but I'm not allowed to before Sunday."

Mr. Pratt looked startled and then laughed. "That's a deal then. Today we'll mind our own business, and tomorrow we'll celebrate."

To my surprise he leaned over and gave me a hug. "I'm glad you're so happy," he said. "I was afraid it might be a problem. Now I'll shut up."

Utopia could tell something had happened, too. When she ran up to the van she took one look at my face and cried, "Oh, what is it? Tell me, quick!"

I held my finger to my lips. "Shhh! Not now. Wait until we're alone."

After Utopia and Mr. Pratt had settled all the business of the shopping list (apparently Hector Graybeal had been complaining that store-bought tobacco evaporated in the pouch), she and I hurried to the barn. While I caught my breath and tried to extract two squashed Milky Ways from my jeans pockets, she fiddled with the dials of my transistor, now kept permanently in the secret room along with her library, which I had recently stocked with Nancy Drews.

"Your devils are sleepy today," she said, shaking the radio impatiently. "Listen to them drawl! Do you think it would help if we dunked them in a pail of cold water?"

"Don't you dare!" I said. "All it needs is new batteries. Here, I'll show you."

I pried open a little lid and extracted two AA batteries. "They wear out, believe it or not," I told her, slipping them into my pocket. "I'll bring some new ones next time I come."

Utopia looked bewildered, but she shrugged. I had revealed so many miracles in the past few months that nothing surprised her anymore. As far as the batteries were concerned, she had only one question: "Shouldn't we bury them, at least?"

I stared. "Bury the batteries? What for?"

"When those poor little devils are dead, do you bury them, or do you just toss them away and use new ones?"

"We toss them away, of course," I said. "What's the use of burying dead batteries?"

Utopia's eyes filled with tears. "I love you dearly, Zannah, and I don't pretend to understand your world, but I'm thankful that in mine, at least, we have more compassion."

"Oh, for heaven's sake!" I spluttered. "You're getting to be as bad as Lafayette. Listen, I'll explain about batteries later. I've got something more important to tell you. This is going to blow your mind!"

Utopia put down the transistor radio and leaned forward expectantly, her eyes glowing. "What is it? Hurry up and tell!"

I took a deep breath and let it out again. It was such an important occasion that I could hardly bring myself to say the words. "We're sisters now, Utopia! Or almost. My mother is going to marry your father—and they're going to announce their engagement tomorrow!"

After a moment of startled disbelief, Utopia smiled. "Really, Zannah? Do you know for a fact?"

"She won't say it yet," I admitted. "She promised someone not to tell until tomorrow. Your father, probably. Maybe he wants to tell you all during family prayers."

Utopia frowned. "That would be unlike Father. But of course, it's unlike Father to want to marry your mother, if it comes to that. She's fabulastic, but I would have thought she was too—I don't know how to explain—too outlandish for him."

I was a little disappointed: I had expected more enthusiasm from Utopia. "Well, love conquers all," I reminded her optimistically. "In a good marriage a couple isn't supposed to be like identical twins; they're supposed to complete each other. I read that the other day in 'Dear Abby.' "

"What's The Rabby?" asked Utopia.

It struck me that we ought to celebrate, but I had forgotten to bring Utopia her latest lesson in twentieth-century food: a pizza. How infuriating to think that it was still sitting in the freezer back home! It would have been perfect for a celebration.

"Oh well," I said after apologizing to Utopia. "It'll keep. How about if we make fudge?"

We had the kitchen to ourselves. The three little boys were cleaning up the barn, Hector Graybeal and Mrs. Noah had gone to inspect fences after last month's big snow, and Shem had disappeared on business of his own. Utopia and I were able to discuss our future freely while we assembled the ingredients for fudge.

"Two cups of sugar, one cup of milk, two squares of chocolate, and a pinch of salt," I rattled off quickly. I had made it so often that I knew the recipe by heart. "We'll need butter, too, but not until the end."

"I don't think we have chocolate," Utopia said doubtfully. "Mr. Pratt brought some at Christmas, but if there was any left over, Loyal would have eaten it by now."

We hunted in the storeroom, but she was right: no chocolate.

"Never mind, we can make brown sugar fudge," I said. "But when I move in here with Patty, I'm going to help you make out the shopping lists. There are a lot of good things you don't even know about."

"I'm not sure Father would like that," Utopia said as she measured out a cup of milk. "You know how he is about new-fangled ideas."

"Well, between Patty's newfangled ideas and your father's old-fashioned ideas, they ought to make an ideal couple," I said, stirring. "No, don't worry, let it boil. It has to get to the soft-ball stage, you know."

"Oh, Zannah!" Utopia cried suddenly. "When you're my sister and we share a room, do you think we could share our clothes, too? We're the same size."

"Sure!" I said. "Have you got some butter handy? If we don't throw it in at exactly the right time, this stuff will fudge and it'll be too late."

The air thickened with a tempting, sugary aroma. If the boys smelled it I knew their tongues would be hanging out, so I wasn't a bit surprised when Shem burst into the kitchen.

"Watch out, don't touch!" I warned him as he approached the stove. "You'll burn your fingers."

Then I saw by his face that he hadn't even noticed the fudge, and I was frightened. I had seen Shem look unfriendly, and I had known him to threaten me, but somehow this was worse. Dropping the spoon, I backed quickly away and moved so that the table was between us.

"What's the matter? What's wrong now?"

Shem's green eyes glinted like snakes' eyes in his pale face. "You!" he said softly, in a controlled voice that I had never heard him use before. "*You're* wrong, Zannah. You made me like you for a while, but that was only witchcraft. You tried to have power over me the way your mother tried to have power over

Mr. Graybeal, but I'm going to stop both of you. I heard every word just now, and in the hayloft, too."

I tried to remember what I had said when I was telling Utopia about Patty marrying her father. Then my mind flashed back to the time I had played my transistor for her, and Shem had known the words to "Credit Card" later the same evening. So he *had* been spying on us! Those noises in the hayloft hadn't been cats and owls; they were Shem. Why wasn't I more careful? Why hadn't I warned Utopia? But above all, why was Shem so angry?

"Okay, so you spied on us," I said. "That's a nasty habit. *We* should be mad, not you. But why can't we be friends? What's wrong with Patty and Mr. Graybeal getting married?"

Shem narrowed his eyes and grew paler than ever. "They're not getting married. You and your mother aren't coming back anymore—not ever! You know what we do with witches?"

I was trembling, but I tried to keep my voice steady. "That's ridiculous, Shem! We're not witches and you know it."

"You're witches, and I can prove it," said Shem. "I have your box, the box with the singing devils. I've hidden it in a safe place. If you go away and stay away, I won't make trouble. But if either of you ever sets foot in these parts again, I'll show Mr. Graybeal, and he'll—he'll exorcise you!"

I tried to laugh. "Utopia—tell him it isn't true! Make him see!"

But Utopia had sunk into a chair with her hands over her eyes. Judging by her quivering shoulders, she was crying.

Suddenly I was burning up with fury. "Oh, you dummy!" I shouted. "You stupid dummy! I might have *known* you'd ruin everything!"

Slamming the door behind me I ran out of the kitchen, dashed across the barnyard, and scrambled up the ladder to the loft. I was vaguely hoping that the radio was still there, hidden behind the Nancy Drews.

Shem had been making no idle threats. It was gone. The

books were still there; if it was true that Shem couldn't read, it wouldn't have occurred to him to use them as another weapon against us. I hid the whole collection under a pile of sacks in the feed room, however. Utopia was in trouble enough already.

What a crazy bunch of people, I thought as I walked out of the barn, still fuming. Red candles were wicked; jeans were an abomination in the eyes of the Lord; even ordinary hairpins were frills and farfelews. Why did life have to be so serious? Were they really so afraid Mr. Rudge would come back and punish them if they didn't behave? No wonder Utopia liked to hide in the loft with a Nancy Drew, and Shem slipped away to the woods from time to time to puff on a pipe and bargain with God.

I caught my breath suddenly. Shem's pipe! Did he still keep it bundled up in that hole in the tree? If so, wouldn't the hole come to mind as a safe hiding place for my transistor, too? Without returning to the house for my down jacket for fear Shem would see me and try to follow, I hurried across the meadow toward the wood.

The snow was long gone. Since that January storm, the ground had thawed twice and twice refrozen. Long shards of ice had become encrusted into the bare earth of the furrows, and as my feet stumbled along I kept slipping and bruising my ankles.

It was cold. My chest and back felt warm from running, but the wind cut through the worn cotton of my jeans, and my ears ached unbearably. By the time I got to the tree, my hands were almost too numb to grip the branches. With the last of my strength I slung myself up, panting and swearing at Shem, tears making hot trickles down my cheeks. I found the hole in the trunk, thrust my arm in and explored every inch of it. But I couldn't find a thing.

I'm not sure which happened first, my foot slipping or Shem's voice shouting. In fact I don't remember much at all about those last moments: only my helpless terror as I fell.

CHAPTER 10

T HE FIRST THING that made any sense to me was the shape of the transistor in my hand. Then other facts came into focus: that my hand was warm, and under something soft—that I was lying on a sofa—that my arm hurt.

Next I noticed voices. Hector Graybeal was somewhere near, and my mother, and Mr. Pratt. I kept my eyes closed while I tried to think. Had I fallen from the tree? Yes, I must have fallen, but where was I now? And why was I holding the transistor?

When I opened my eyes, the first face I saw was Shem's. It was as white as chalk. Moving a little closer, he managed a nervous smile. "So you're not dead?"

I tried to shake my head, but it hurt too much. "I'm alive, you dummy. No thanks to you!"

"Hush, Zannah," said Patty, coming forward to smooth my forehead. "It's thanks to Shem that you're here at all, instead of freezing to death out in the woods. What got into you, going off like that without your jacket? If you had to climb a tree, couldn't you have chosen a closer one? Anyone would think you were *trying* to kill yourself. It's lucky for you that Shem followed and brought you home!"

Her voice ended with a wail, and Mr. Pratt put his arm around her and left it there. "She's all right, Patty," he said. "She got a bad bump and a broken arm, but it could have been a lot worse. We'll take her back to Georgetown Hospital and have her patched up, and she'll be as good as ever."

"Shem brought me home?" I whispered. "You mean he carried me?"

Shem turned scarlet. "No trouble," he said awkwardly. "And I saw to it you got what you were looking for."

I didn't understand what made him give it back, but I nodded, still clutching my transistor under the covers.

"In any case, there's no use wearing you out with questions," Patty said shakily. "I suppose it'll all make sense later. But it sure came as a shock, let me tell you. Here Peter and I were turning up to announce our good news, and we found Hector and Marigold waiting at the door, looking like death."

"Good news?" I repeated. "Yours and Mr. Pratt's? *What* good news?"

In spite of my aching head, I propped myself up and looked from face to face. Utopia, who was hovering in the background, shrugged and gave me a rueful little smile.

"Don't you remember?" said Patty. "We're getting married!"

I couldn't believe my ears. "Married! You and Mr. Pratt? But that's not what I thought you meant—that's all wrong!"

Patty sat down on the bed and hugged me. "Oh, dear—I thought you guessed long ago! But it'll be all right, you'll see. You and I have had good years together, Zannah, but with three of us, we'll be happier than ever."

They certainly looked happy. It was enough to make a person cry. And no one else seemed to mind at all, including Shem. In fact, Shem looked positively joyful.

"What are you grinning about?" I asked him crossly.

"Good news," he said. "Good for them, too," and he crooked his thumb at his mother and Mr. Graybeal. "I know what you wanted, but it wouldn't have worked because those two belong together."

"You and I have had good years together, Zannah, but with three of us, we'll be happier than ever."

Mrs. Noah gasped, glanced about wildly, and ran her fingers through her hair. "Oh, Shem—what do you mean? You know I wouldn't dream—that is, we wouldn't dare—that is—oh, Hector, what can I say?"

Shifting his weight from side to side, Hector Graybeal tugged at his beard. He looked miserable. "Woman, thy name is loquacity!" he mumbled.

Shem clenched his fists and scowled at him. "It's not, and it wouldn't be Rudge either, if you two had any sense. It would be Marigold Graybeal."

There was a moment of shocked silence before Mrs. Noah burst into tears and ran from the room.

"Well!" said Patty. "I don't know what that was all about, but now isn't the time to find out. Go hitch up the mare, Peter, and Utopia—see if you can find a couple of blankets and a pillow or two. We don't want Zannah jounced around any more than we can help on the way home."

The crowd disappeared, or so it seemed until I noticed that Shem still lingered by the door. Patty eyed him severely, but instead of leaving, he edged back into the room.

"Need to talk to Zannah," he said gruffly.

Patty shook her head. "Zannah is too weak to talk now, Shem. Maybe in a day or so."

But he moved forward stubbornly. "Need to explain. I won't make Zannah talk."

Patty gave a sigh of exasperation and walked over to the window to watch for Mr. Pratt and the van.

I just stared at Shem, trying to figure him out. That same morning he had looked as if he'd like to kill me. Now his face was practically affectionate. And what was the story with the transistor? He had said he needed to explain, but he kept standing there, pale and mute.

"Well?" I said softly. "If you want to say something, better say it fast. We're going home."

Shem cleared his throat. "You understand," he muttered.

"No," I said firmly. Shem, at his best, had never been very articulate, but he was going to have to do better than this.

"I knew it would happen, you see," said Shem. "That is, I knew it *could* happen, given time, and I thought it would be the best thing for—well, for everybody."

I waited.

"It's not that I didn't like you," he added shyly, "but when I heard you tell Utopia that your mother would marry Mr. Graybeal—"

"Sorry about that," I said. "I was a little off course. Patty had ideas of her own."

"First place," said Shem with a chortle, "he wouldn't call her 'Patty.' He'd call her 'Woman'!"

I moaned. "Don't make me laugh. I ache all over."

Shem pulled a solemn face. "What I meant to say—I suppose you're not witches—"

"Gee, thanks!" I said.

"But that box—" he continued. "I heard it sing, up in the loft. Only, when I took it, it wouldn't sing anymore. Why did it work for you and not for me?"

I knew why: I had taken out the batteries. But I wasn't about to let Shem lure me away from the point.

"Never mind that. What I want to know is why you took it in the first place. This whole thing is ridiculous. If there was something going on between Mr. Graybeal and your mother, you could have told me. I'm reasonable. I might even have helped. I'll help now, if you'll just—"

Patty turned from the window and strode back across the room. "You said you wouldn't make her talk," she told Shem accusingly. "It seems to me Zannah is the only one holding forth."

"Oh, don't fuss," I said, reaching for her hand. "This is important! You and Mr. Pratt are happy now—there ought to be something we can do for Shem's mother and Mr. Graybeal."

"Do for them?" said Patty. "They seem to be doing pretty well for themselves. And Shem was right: they belong together."

Shem nodded. "Stands to reason Mother is a widow, or just as good as, the way my father used witchcraft to move the dairy."

He leaned toward Patty confidentially. "If you ask me, we're all better off than before. If only we could be sure he leaves us here, and doesn't—doesn't come to make more trouble."

Patty groaned, but she looked sympathetic. "You mean they don't feel free to marry? The poor sweeties! Well, I don't want any more talking, and that's final. But I promise we'll come back and help. And don't worry, Shem: I have an idea!"

It took a while to get it all straight. When you've fixed it in your head that things are going to happen a certain way, it's not easy to accept the fact that they're altogether different. My headache didn't help matters. I felt sick and dizzy all the way back in the van, and Patty was in too much of a dither at Georgetown Hospital for me to get a word in edgewise.

Once the doctors had assured her that I was okay, she bustled me home and tucked me into bed with a cup of hot milk and honey. "Try to sleep," she ordered, backing out of my room.

"Hey, wait a minute!" I said. "Just one thing."

She came back in and looked at me innocently.

"Are you sure you want to be 'Patty Pratt'?" I asked.

"Of course!" said Patty. "Can you think of a better name?"

I shrugged. "I had kind of planned on 'Patty Graybeal.' "

Patty looked as if she were going to laugh, but she managed to keep a straight face. "I think we both fell in love the same day, Zannah," she said. "You fell in love with the Hunky-Dory Dairy, and I fell in love with Peter."

"First sight?" I asked.

Patty nodded. "First sight."

I sighed. "Oh, well—then it's good things turned out the way they did, and I guess I put Shem to a lot of unnecessary trouble. So first thing tomorrow, you be sure and tell me your idea for his mother and Mr. Graybeal."

CHAPTER 11

I STAYED IN bed all day Sunday, and by Monday morning I was feeling like a normal, although slightly battered human being again. A knock on my bedroom door woke me up at around nine, and I was startled to see Mr. Pratt walk in, carrying a tray.

"Compliments of the dairy staff," he announced. "Mrs. Noah outdid herself. Better tuck right in, though. I may not have done such a great job heating it up."

I lifted a checkered dishcloth and saw my favorite dairy breakfast: coffee, sausage, fried apples, and homemade biscuits with jam. On the side, floating in a teacup, was a single primrose.

I leaned forward to sniff at the yellow petals. "Already? In February?"

"Shem found it," said Mr. Pratt. "First of the season. He said it brings good luck."

"He should have kept it, then," I said, stuffing a biscuit into my mouth. "He needs it more than I do."

I scooped a dribble of jam from my chin and licked it off my finger. Then I took a second look at Mr. Pratt. He was dressed in jeans and a ragged sweatshirt, with his dairy cap cocked jauntily over one ear.

"Aren't you going to be late for work?"

"Quit my job," he said. "It's a good thing I did. Your mother has a headache. I told her to go back to bed, I'd handle the kids by myself today."

I sat bolt upright, sloshing coffee all over the fried apples. "Oh, my God, that's true—it's Monday! And Lafayette quit *her* job, too. What are we going to do?"

"Calm down," Mr. Pratt advised me. "And go easy on that arm—you don't want another trip to the emergency room. The kids are doing fine. I gave them a project to keep them quiet for a few minutes."

"What project?" I asked suspiciously.

"A desert rodent, called a gerbil," he told me with a proud smile. "A friend donated it to the cause. Ever seen one? It's a little mousy thing with a long tail."

"Oh, no!" I wailed. "Not gerbils!"

"One gerbil, Zannah," he said patiently. "Only one."

"There is no such thing as one gerbil," I informed him. "I can just see it: gerbils in the kitchen, gerbils in the closets, itty-bitty droppings all over the house—what did I do to deserve this?"

"Don't panic," said Mr. Pratt. "It's in a cage. At least, it will be when the kids are finished with it. Nature studies, you know. Told them to pass it around, see what they could tell me about it when I came back."

"Finished with it?" I shuddered. "Finished is right. One defenseless little gerbil and twenty-four Tinies? I should report you to the Humane Society!"

"Actually, there are only twenty-three kids today," Mr. Pratt told me seriously. "Zippo is absent."

I gave him a long, pitying look. "It's a good thing you don't have to do this every day. You have a lot to learn."

"But I do have to," he said, picking up my tray. "That is, I chose to. Didn't Patty tell you? I'm the new assistant."

It was news to me and I had a lot to say on the subject, but before I could start, we heard a distant but earsplitting scream.

"Better get moving," I said. "I think maybe that was the death cry of the desert rodent."

After he left, I tried to sit tight and enjoy myself. It isn't every day you get to stay home from school when you're in a state to enjoy it. But my curiosity got the better of me. I threw down my book, pulled on some clothes (no easy feat with a broken arm), and set off to see how Mr. Pratt was coping with the Tinies. I met him on the stairs, halfway down to the group's newly remodeled playroom. He was gingerly carrying a paper bag.

"Is that the corpse?" I asked. "Here, give it to me. I'll take it out and bury it."

"Sweet of you, Zannah," he said, handing me the bag. "You're all consideration today. I appreciate that."

But when I looked in the bag, I found that it contained a pair of pink-flowered Carter's underpants. Wet.

"Thanks," I said. "Whose are these, by the way? Or shouldn't I ask?"

"They belong to Becky. I was going to consult your mother, but now I won't have to disturb her. What's the procedure?"

"They've all got extras in their cubbyholes," I told him. "You know, where they keep their lunch boxes. Have you noticed how it's always Zippo who needs to go to the bathroom, but it's Becky who wets her pants?"

"Zippo is absent today," said Mr. Pratt.

I started upstairs with the paper bag, but a thought struck me. "What was that scream?"

"They were *all* screaming," said Mr. Pratt, looking a little dazed. "The gerbil got away, and they couldn't find him. The kids figured he'd head straight for food, so they dumped their lunch boxes out on the floor, and that included the contents of their thermos bottles. He wasn't there, so they tried to pack up again. The screaming was due to a difference of opinion over the ownership of desserts."

"Thanks for making it clear," I said. "Did you ever find the gerbil?"

"Yes," said Mr. Pratt. "He was hiding in his cage."

I decided he could do with a little moral support, so after throwing Becky's pants in the washer, I joined him in the playroom. The first thing I saw was the desert rodent, happily spinning round and round in his exercise wheel. The Tinies were seated in a big semicircle on the floor, staring with adoration at their new assistant, who had written the following information on the blackboard:

WHAT DID WE FIND OUT ABOUT GERBILS?
1. Gerbils are cute.
2. Gerbils are furry.
3. Gerbils have a tail but if you
   try to hold them by it they will
   shinny up it and bite you.
4. Gerbils don't care where they pee.

"Mr. Pratt," I whispered, edging up close to him. "I don't want to hurt your feelings or anything, but the Tinies can't read."

Ignoring me, he pointed at a kid in purple overalls who was raising his hand. "Did you think of something else, Jamie?"

"Gerbils are a pain in the neck," said Jamie. "My dad told me."

Mr. Pratt wrote, "5. Gerbils are a pain in the neck," on the blackboard, while the class looked on approvingly.

"Okay," he said. "Now we're all going to take turns drawing a picture of a gerbil on the blackboard, and the best picture gets a prize."

Jamie raised his hand again. "What's the prize?"

"The prize," said Mr. Pratt, "is that the winner gets to take home the gerbil."

I relaxed. Peter Pratt was obviously a natural for preschool child care. He had been wasting his talents in a nine-to-five office job. Closing the playroom door gently behind me, I tiptoed back upstairs to pay a visit to my mother.

Patty was lying in semidarkness with the radio turned on low. She smiled at me when I peeked around the door, and beckoned me in. "How is Peter doing?"

"Not bad," I said. "In fact, I think he's a real find. Let's just hope he doesn't chicken out."

"He won't," said Patty. "He says compared to his office, this place is heaven."

"They say love is blind," I commented. "Which reminds me, what was your idea about Mr. Graybeal and Mrs. Noah?"

"The pure and honest truth," said Patty. "We've been treating those people as if the truth would kill them. But they've been through every kind of hardship: poverty, and sickness, and fear, to say nothing of witchcraft. The truth would be a blessing, compared to all of that."

"Maybe," I said doubtfully, "but I still don't see how it would solve their problem."

Patty turned off the radio. "I'm not saying it would solve their problem, but it might appease their consciences to know that Rudge was dead. My idea was to come up with some evidence. Peter has a friend who works at the *Washington Post*. They have all the obituaries on file, and I thought he could look up Rudge."

I nodded hopefully.

"Well, I'm sorry, Zannah, but it didn't work."

"You mean he didn't die?"

"Of course he died," Patty said impatiently. "It just wasn't mentioned in the *Post*. But figure it out for yourself: Shem is thirteen, right? Say his father was twenty-five when Shem was born—and chances are he was older—he would have been thirty-three when the dairy was removed. That was in 1880, which would make him one hundred and thirty-nine years old today. He's dead all right, but we've got to prove it. I've been thinking about those old experimental communities. If we tracked down the right one, we might find they buried their dead on their own land. Most of those old cemetaries still exist, and a photo of the tombstone would convince Hector and Marigold. It'll involve some research, of course."

"It's worth a try," I admitted. "When can we start?"

Patty yawned, rolled over, and buried her head in the pillow. "One of these days. We can start by exploring the countryside casually on weekends. It would be fun. And we could make a real project of it over Easter vacation. Be an angel, Zannah, and bring me a cup of tea. Then with luck I can pry myself out of bed."

I went down to the kitchen, put the kettle on, and rinsed the breakfast coffee out of Patty's favorite mug. I found a tea bag and put three cookies on a plate. And all the time I was grumbling to myself. One of these days? Casually on weekends? Easter vacation? But Hector Graybeal and Mrs. Noah were worried *now*, frightened *now*, in love *now*. Patty, of all people, ought to understand that. How could I go back to the dairy and tell Shem "one of these days"?

I opened the kitchen door and stood looking out into the backyard. The ground had thawed again, but nowhere was there any sign of spring. Still, the air was mild and humid with a hint of hope in it, as there often is in Washington toward the end of February. Off to the northwest, a flock of crows circled in the blustery sky over treetops that might be the beginning of Archbold Glover Park. The Hunky-Dory Dairy felt so near, yet with the threat of being far away. Weekends? Easter? Not for me. I was going to help those people *now*.

When I delivered Patty's tea and cookies, I rummaged in her closet for a shawl. It was hard enough buttoning a shirt around my cast; I wasn't going to attempt zipping myself into a down jacket. Remembering Utopia's instructions, I crossed the shawl over my chest, hooked the ends around my waist, and managed to tie a clumsy knot.

Over Patty's black cocktail dress the fluffy wool looked gorgeous. On me it looked like a gigantic bandage. But the material made an ample pocket in front, and into that pocket I stuffed what evidence I could find, at short notice, of the time I lived in. There was the "Metro" section of the *Washington Post* from January 1, the day Lafayette's baby was born. There was this year's calendar, with Garfield saying something silly at the top of every month. There was my class photo with the year clearly printed on the sign that read, "Sixth Grade—Ms. Randall's Homeroom," and there was a bottle of Stress-Formula vitamin pills, stamped "Expires September, 1987."

After checking that the coast was clear, I crept out of the house, and in order to avoid further delay, pedaled furiously through Burleith on my old dirt bike. Believe it or not, a broken arm is not an obstacle to riding a bicycle. It's no worse than carrying an armful of books or sipping a soft drink while you ride along. The track through the woods was hazardous, but I made it safely and tumbled off amid a squawking panic of chickens in the barnyard, just as Hector Graybeal, Mrs. Noah, and all five children filed out the kitchen door.

First came Utopia, whose face lit up when she saw me. Shem followed. He looked glad to see me, but I could tell that once he caught sight of my dirt bike, I no longer existed for him. The little boys rushed after him as he strode across the barnyard to inspect the heap of pedals and reflectors and spinning wheels.

Hector Graybeal was no less intrigued by the sight, but his face was forbidding. As for Mrs. Noah, she had eyes for nothing but me.

"Zannah!" she cried, and very carefully, as if she thought I would shatter, she kissed me.

"Yes, it's me—Zannah McFee!" I said firmly, slipping out of her embrace. "And this is the year of our Lord, *nineteen*-eighty-seven!"

I showed them everything, told them everything, watched their eyes open as they battled disbelief. For one glorious hour I was the bearer of good news. I thought I had solved their problem and broken the spell. But in spite of their eventual polite acceptance of the fact that years had passed, and God-fearing men now flew through the air and watched scandalous theatricals in little glowing boxes from the comfort of their own parlors, nothing really changed. They were still afraid.

"But Mr. Rudge is dead!" I shouted. "If he were alive today, he'd be at least a hundred and thirty-nine years old, and no one lives that long."

Then I looked at their faces and saw that they didn't believe me.

I sighed. My arm started to ache again, and I wished I had stayed where I belonged, in my own warm bed. I felt an irrepressible urge to run back to Patty and howl. But before I gave way to it, I had one more try.

"What do you plan to do, then?" I asked them wearily. "Just go on being scared? What kind of life is that? If you want to be happy, you have to risk *something*, you know. But what you do is none of my business. I'm going to take my bicycle and go home."

I thought I had left them all behind, standing in a sad little group, dazed by what I had just said. But as I had my foot on the pedal and was about to shove off, I felt a gentle touch on my shoulder.

"So that's a bicycle!" said Mrs. Noah with an impish smile.

I scowled. "It sure is. One day you might get your nerve up to put on a pair of jeans and learn to ride it."

She shook her head in total disbelief, but then suddenly she stopped smiling. "Zannah," she said, "I need Hector like a fish needs a bicycle, so I'm going to see to it that he takes your advice. I'm going to see to it we *all* do."

I was a little confused for a while. Did she mean she didn't need Hector Graybeal, or did she really think a fish could use a bicycle? It wasn't until my next visit that I figured it out. She and Mr. Graybeal were holding hands a lot, and the whole bunch of them at the dairy looked a bit more relaxed. A bit, but not totally. Because in spite of the happy ending, our troubles were not all solved.

For instance, even now that Hector Graybeal and Mrs. Noah consider themselves free to marry, they haven't yet found a preacher to marry them. Peter Pratt, who, I found out only when he quit his job, was a lawyer, has been trying to explain to them about common-law marriages.

I'll never understand why he wanted to throw over a classy job with good pay just to help Patty run the Tiny Fingers Pre-school Playgroup, but as an assistant, Peter has it all over Lafayette. Now the playgroup has turned into a small school. The three of us moved to a bigger house in Burleith, and we have thirty-six Tinies instead of twenty-four. Knowing Peter and Patty, there's nothing to keep us from expanding. They have three full-time helpers, but that's still not enough to mop up all the purple paint.

I'd help them pull the place together if I had time, but I'm much too busy. Utopia and I have our hands full, teaching Shem and the little boys to read, out at the Hunky-Dory Dairy.

A CAST OF CHARACTERS
TO DELIGHT THE HEARTS
OF READERS!

BUNNICULA   51094-4/$2.50
James and Deborah Howe, illustrated by Alan Daniel
The now-famous story of the vampire bunny, this ALA
Notable Book begins the light-hearted story of the small
rabbit the Monroe family find in a shoebox at a Dracula
film. He looks like any ordinary bunny to Harold the dog.
But Chester, a well-read and observant cat, is suspicious
of the newcomer, whose teeth strangely resemble
fangs...

HOWLIDAY INN   69294-5/$2.50
James Howe, illustrated by Lynn Munsinger
"Another hit for the author of BUNNICULA!"
                                    School Library Journal
The continued "tail" of Chester the cat and Harold the
dog as they spend their summer vacation at the foreboding
Chateau Bow-Wow, a kennel run by a mad scientist!

THE CELERY STALKS AT MIDNIGHT   69054-3/$2.50
James Howe, illustrated by Leslie Morrill
Bunnicula is back and on the loose in this third hilarious
novel featuring Chester the cat, Harold the dog, and the
famous vampire bunny. This time Bunnicula is missing
from his cage, and Chester and Harold turn sleuth to find
him, and save the town from a stalk of bloodless celery!
"Expect surprises. Plenty of amusing things happen."
                           The New York Times Book Review

AVON Camelot Paperbacks